M

Centenary Collection

**Celebrating 100 years of romance with
the very best of Mills & Boon**

*First published in Great Britain 2008
by Harlequin Mills & Boon Limited,
Eton House, 18-24 Paradise Road, Richmond, Surrey TW9 1SR*

© Margaret Way, Pty, Ltd. 2001

ISBN: 978 0 263 86621 6

77-1008

*Harlequin Mills & Boon policy is to use papers that are
natural, renewable and recyclable products and made from
wood grown in sustainable forests. The logging and
manufacturing processes conform to the legal environmental
regulations of the country of origin.*

*Printed and bound in Spain
by Litografia Rosés S.A., Barcelona*

Genni's Dilemma

by
Margaret Way

MILLS & BOON
Pure reading pleasure

Margaret Way takes great pleasure in her work and works hard at her pleasure. She enjoys tearing off to the beach with her family at weekends, loves haunting galleries and auctions and is completely given over to French champagne 'for every possible joyous occasion'. sShe was born and educated in the river city of Brisbane, Australia, and now lives within sight and sound of beautiful Moreton Bay.

CHAPTER ONE

The Wedding Eve

GENEVIEVE stood outside her mother's bedroom door bracing herself for the inevitable confrontation and, she guessed, copious tears. Angel was perfectly capable of it. Generally believed saccharine-sweet, no one knew better than Angel how to make a lot of people uncomfortable. She could turn it on. And off. At the flip of a coin.

Genevieve didn't know if she could stand it, feeling as bad as she did. After a month of agonizing about this soon-to-be-taken trip to the altar, she had lost weight to the point she was looking more spindly than slim; she had a permanent headache; she was sick to her stomach and trying to smile through it; her emotions so barely under control it hurt.

About to tap on the door and await entrée into her mother's opulent bedroom that stopped just short of mirrors on the ceiling, Genevieve suddenly remembered with a great sense of relief Angel was going out to dinner with Toby Slocombe. She marvelled she could have forgotten, but then her brain was firing on less than four cylinders.

Toby was one of the high rollers around Sydney Town, recently divorced from his long-suffering wife of thirty years. For once Angel hadn't been involved having just come out of a rather unsettling experience with a toy-boy a little older than her daughter. So tonight no tears to spoil the mascara. No tears to stain Angel's ravishing little heart-shaped face. Even so she wouldn't take it without a bit of light screaming and the usual attempt to talk Genevieve down. Genevieve felt she could just about endure that. Angel's soft breathy voice raised a few decibels arguing nonstop. No one was home except Genevieve's beloved Emmy, their long-time housekeeper, baby-sitter, nanny, confidante, social secretary-assistant, referee, who had been more of a mother to Genevieve than Angel the perennial beauty and social butterfly had ever been.

This is supposed to be one of the happiest days of my life, Genevieve thought, avoiding all self-pity. Indeed she felt very isolated and quite guilty, tempted to do a runner. Please God help me through this, she prayed as she rapped on her mother's door, the great emerald-cut diamond on her left hand winking and blinking heavy enough to anchor a harbour ferry.

"Come!" her mother's voice trilled.

It was the sort of response one might expect from a celebrated prima donna, not a mother, Genevieve thought. Not a "Come in" much less "Yes, darling." Emmy, after all, was watching one of her favourite TV shows, not surprisingly, "The Nanny," and could not be disturbed. Not knowing whether to laugh or cry Genevieve opened the door, her eyes filled with the sight of her mother half falling out of a long sequinned evening dress in a heavenly shade of jacaranda that must have cost as much as the piece of antique furniture Genevieve was about to bump into.

"Lordy, Sweet Mamma," she said, amazed like everyone else by her mother's youthful appearance and all-out glamour.

Angel, the picture of seduction, threw out her slender arms and made a full turn. "Like it?"

"What there is of it, yes," Genevieve agreed slowly. "It's beautiful. Exquisite."

"I'd let you wear it only you're too tall," Angel instantly responded, smoothing the filmy fabric over her hips.

"I'm not *that* tall," Genevieve said. "Anyway, you've never lent me anything."

Angel sprayed herself with another whiff of gorgeous perfume. "Genni, sweetheart, you've never wanted for anything. I know you're beautiful, though I looked twice as good when I was your age, but you have your poor father's height. And that olive skin." Angel turned to survey her own flawless strawberries-and-cream complexion.

"Most people think my skin is great," Genevieve answered casually enough. She always took her mother's little put-downs with no offence. "Unlike you, I take a tan and it goes very well with my hair."

"Our hair," Angel corrected, touching her heavy white-gold naturally wavy locks. In her mid-forties, an age Angel kept quite secret even from her doctor, Angel wore her hair short, brushed up and away from her exceedingly youthful, marvellously pretty face. Genevieve wore hers long, sheets of it, falling to her shoulder blades. Sometimes she had it straightened but it inevitably went back into its waving skeins.

The two of them were very much alike despite the fact Angel was petite and Genevieve stood 5'8" in her stockinged feet with long, light limbs. Most people thought Genevieve was twice as beautiful as her mother and as a member of the Courtland family it was expected she would have brains, something her mother either didn't have or concealed. Not that it affected Angel's great ongoing success with men. In fact it might well have contributed to it.

"Genni, do you know what you're doing?" Angel broke sharply into her daughter's reverie.

"Nope, what am I doing?" Genevieve asked.

"You're handling that precious piece of Sevres so carelessly you might drop it. Please put it down."

"Sorry, Mamma."

"Darling, haven't I asked you not to call me that?"

Genevieve laughed, trying to cloak a lifetime's despair. "You're one tough lady, Angel. Do you know that? You asked me not to call you Mamma when I was barely ten years old. Not all that long after Daddy died." It was cruel. Genevieve still thought it was cruel but she had never been one to start, in her own words, "a ruckus." Not being able to call her mother Mummy or Mum had not only been harrowing, it had somehow affected their relationship. Underneath it all Genevieve felt terrible sorrow her mother wasn't the complete woman.

In fact Angel was moaning now. "Oh, don't start that again." She always did at any mention of her late first husband, Genevieve's father, Stephen Courtland. Angel had divorced Stephan when Genevieve was seven. Eighteen months later he had been tragically killed in a shooting accident on Jubilee. Jubilee was the Courtland flagship, the desert fortress and ancestral home. The Courtlands controlled a cattle empire that cut a huge swathe through the giant state of Queensland. Blaine was the current custodian of the flame. Blaine Courtland, Genevieve's kissin' cousin, prince among men.

At thirty-one, handsome as the devil and just as arrogant, he was a much respected man in a tough man's world. Blaine had been the hero of Genevieve's childhood and early adolescence. Eight whole years separated them but they were light years away in substance and maturity.

The little girl Blaine had always called by a string of endearments: flower face, Violetta—because of her eyes—sweetness, cherub, little pal, even pumpkin—she remembered all of them—overnight turned into that silly little idiot Genni who was prepared to waste her perfectly good brain trying to emulate her fool of a mother. Blaine pulled no punches about Angel. He actually called her Jinx to her face. A lot of it stemmed from the fact the Courtland family collectively believed Stephen Courtland's "accident" had been no accident at all. Everyone knew Stephen had been devastated when Angel walked out on him, taking his adored only child. A serious depression had followed.

"Angel, can I talk to you?" Genevieve asked, picking up her courage.

"I don't really have time to talk now, darling," Angel said, hunting up her exquisite evening purse, popping in a fragile lace-edged hanky. "Shouldn't you be getting your beauty sleep? It's going to be a wonderful day tomorrow. I'm so proud of you landing Colin."

Genevieve received a mind picture of Blaine so searing it hurt her head. "I think I'll pass on Colin," she blurted abruptly.

"You'll what?" Angel's blue-violet eyes started so far from her head she looked like an adorable bug.

"I can't go through with it, Mamma… Angel. I feel terrible about it, I know it's what you want. What you've done everything in your considerable power to bring about, but I don't love Colin. I never did. I was going through with marrying him to spite Blaine. I can see that now."

Angel sat down heavily in a cream damask armchair, her tiny face blanching. "I'm not hearing this. I'm not!" she wailed. "What has this got to do with Blaine? You surely can't believe he'll be pleased about this. He's paid for the whole blasted thing."

She was betrayed. In that moment humiliation left her bereft. "He what?" Her desperation was almost total.

"Oh, don't play the fool. It doesn't work with me," Angel scolded with some contempt. "You surely didn't think I was going to outlay a small fortune. The Courtlands have a mountain of money. Blaine can well afford a lavish wedding for three hundred. A drop in the ocean to him. But it would leave a big dint in my bank balance."

"My God!" Genevieve could have howled with the pain.

"You let me believe you were handling all this, Mother. Yes, *Mother.* You are my mother, aren't you? My father, God rest his soul, left you very well off. He loved you, the poor deluded man. He loved *me.* There has to be money, Mother. Look around this God-awful bedroom, this mansion of a house. Look at that dress you've got on. The diamonds in your ears and around your neck."

"Will you please stop making a commotion?" Angel wrung her hands. "I have to look after *myself,* Genevieve. I have many more years left to me."

"I thought you were working your head off to land Toby Slocombe?" Genevieve fired.

"Don't you dare scream at me, you ungrateful little wretch." Angel was furious and showed it. "How can you possibly let me down? Let Colin down? I don't dare think of the consequences."

"No." Genevieve shook her head violently, in agony. "Because you expected me to help out once I got my hands on the Garrett money. You know Colin's father is universally detested."

"I happen to know he approves of you," Angel said, tight-lipped with anger. "He's thrilled Colin has finally found someone who will be a good steadying influence on him."

"You've played us all like puppets," Genevieve said, recognizing it was true. "You might give some people the impression you're an airhead but you always get what you want, don't you, Mother?"

Angel had the grace to flush. "I don't know what's got into you, Genevieve. You haven't been the same since you got back from Jubilee. Of course it's Blaine. He's always so goddam polite, but I know he hates me. They all do. They blame me for Stephen. As though I was there when he tripped over that bloody fence. They're a revolting family. So uppity. The landed elite. Yet Blaine's own mother ran off. Dear Crystelle. Don't let him fool you. Blaine hates women."

Genevieve brushed a long ash-gold tendril from her face. "He was kindness itself to me."

"You mean when you were a little kid," Angel scoffed, jealous of Blaine's affection for her daughter to this day.

"A little *fatherless* kid. I loved Blaine with all my heart," Genevieve admitted, frightened somehow by the depth of her own emotion.

Angel gave a hard laugh. "Well, that's all gone by the board. You two have had a very difficult relationship for years now. The arrogance of the man! He has always interfered. You'd think he was your guardian, not me. Remember the time I wanted you to be a model. You could have been right up there at the top. An international career. You had everything going for you, but no, Blaine insisted you go on to university."

"I was a straight-A student, Angel," Genevieve reminded her. "I didn't want to be a model."

That struck Angel as irrelevant. "It's the best career a beautiful girl could possibly have. Such an exciting, glamorous life."

"So you say. It wasn't for me."

Angel's pretty mouth puckered. "So working at the State Art Gallery is better?"

"I have a Fine Arts Degree. I'm quite a good artist myself. I'm learning all the time. I'm regarded as a valuable addition to the team. All of this fades into the background now, Angel, I can't go through with this marriage."

That struck Angel as shocking. She burst into faintly hysterical laughter. "Not a chance you're getting out of it," she cried loudly. "Blaine will drag you down the aisle if he has to. Don't forget there's the honour of the Courtland name at stake."

Genevieve's violet eyes burned. "I'm only a cousin, Angel. Third cousin. I don't really count."

"Don't be so sure of that, my girl." Angel began to fiercely swing an evening-sandalled foot. "This would be the most appalling breach of social etiquette. It's unthinkable."

"Except if I go through with it I'll be making the most hideous mistake of my life," Genevieve said in a voice thin with despair. "Please listen to me, Angel. I feel so *alone*. Shaking inside."

But Angel was furious with her. "Who the devil *are* you, Genevieve?" she shouted. "Who are you really? You're certain of it? Why *now*. Why didn't you just leave it until tomorrow morning? Climb out the bathroom window. I know you've seen that movie with Julia Roberts. Jumping on horses. You've got cold feet. All brides have cold feet. A little surprise for you, darling. You simply cannot let any of us down. You're emotionally fragile, like your father."

At that Genevieve's violet eyes flashed into brilliant life. "Damn you, Mamma," she said. "Damn you for leaving my father in the first place. Isn't it enough that he's dead? You're going to defame him?"

"Now just hang on a minute," Angel hissed. "I'm not defaming anyone. I'm saying it the way it is. You started something. Finish it. You're going to go through with this marriage, Genevieve. Colin Garrett is a catch most girls would kill for. He's attractive, he's rich—or he will be, he always makes the best-dressed list, he's more 'in' than 'out' in all the glossies. He's ideal. I just love the way he kisses my fingertips every time he sees me. *Bellisima, Angelina!* he always says."

"Why don't you just tell him to shut up?" Genevieve continued angrily. "His mother won't be unhappy. I know in my heart she doesn't think we're suited. I think she thinks I might desert her darling boy sometime in the future. Like you deserted Daddy." Her voice quivered pathetically.

Angel tilted her head back, staring at the elaborately decorated plaster ceiling. "I didn't desert your father, Genevieve. I just moved out. I've never met a man so *needy* in my whole life. I found his love for me suffocating, his insistence on a 'home life'. The three of us doing things together. God, how dreary! Possessiveness can be pretty awful."

Angel stood up in a torment. "You've upset me, Genevieve," she said. "What a lousy thing to do. I accept you're uptight. It's certainly not unheard of. I strongly advise you have a glass of warm milk and go to bed. When you wake up in the morning you'll feel entirely different." She turned to face her daughter, who somehow looked fourteen years old. "Now, Toby will be here shortly. I don't want to hear any more of this. I can't deal with it. I don't know either why you can't stand the idea of Blaine's paying for it all?"

"That's because you're a sponger, Mamma. You're good at it." Genevieve lifted her head, pinning her mother's gaze. "But I'm going to hold it against you forever."

"Are you?" Angel exploded, sweet voice rasping. "How dare you speak to me like this, Genevieve, you sanctimonious little twit. Blaine and I have been working together for years. He's a very complex character, is your hero. He hasn't approved of anything you've done these last couple of years yet he's more than happy to pick up all your bills.

"Oh, yes, darling, don't look so shocked. It might have been my deepest darkest secret, but Blaine has helped out a lot. Why not? He really did think you were a great little kid and he's notoriously difficult to please. And you're a Courtland. That's a huge thing in your favour. Blaine was happy to keep you in the appropriate manner."

Genevieve felt like a hand was squeezing her heart. "You asked him?"

Incredibly Angel became almost jovial. "Not at all. He just did it. You were the entrancing little 'honey chile'. But I expect by now he'll be happy to let someone else shoulder the burden."

A deep vivid rose stained Genevieve's golden skin. She looked up, her eyes as dark as the ocean, aware as she had never been before in her life deep inside her mother some odd malice moved. "Don't say any more, Angel," she begged. She, too, stood up, straightening her shoulders. "With any sort of luck after tomorrow we mightn't have to see one another again."

Angel heard the finality in her daughter's voice. "Dear, oh, dear, what a silly thing to say," she gushed. "I love you, Genni. I'm very proud of you." She swept forward to pat her daughter's face, wondering why when she was so pretty herself she always felt jealous of Genni's hair, her eyes, her mouth, the radiant smile never much in evidence these days, the lovely teeth. God she even wished she was taller, then she wouldn't have to diet so rigorously.

"The last thing in the world I want is for you to be unhappy, Genni," she said tremulously, ready to shed a few tears. "Trust me, darling, you're suffering from prenuptial nerves. It's normal, not a catastrophe. Colin is so nice. Such fun, and he'll be drowning in money. I've been responsible for you for so long you should feel some responsibility for me. I know tomorrow you're going to make us all very proud. It's my dream, honey."

After her mother had left in a flurry of breathless giggles, hanging on to Toby Slocombe's arm, Genevieve went in search of Emmy. Emmy was still sitting in front of the television in the small room off the library, watching an old movie, a half-eaten box of Belgium chocolates Genevieve had bought for her on her lap, short plump legs resting on an ottoman.

"Hello, darling girl." Emmy looked up to smile; her pleasure diminishing as she saw the anguish in Genevieve's expression. "Going to watch this with me?"

Despite herself Genevieve was amused. "God, Em, you must have seen this movie a hundred times?" She recognised Cary Grant and Eva Marie Saint. *North by Northwest.*

"Better than the ones they make these days," Emmy snorted. "Wasn't he just the handsomest man?"

"He surely was," Genevieve agreed. "Bisexual, I gather?"

"That's just talk." Em snatched up another chocolate. "He was a real man. Anyway, what's wrong with you? You look like you need a stiff drink when you should be looking bliss-fully happy."

Genevieve sat down, gripping her hands. "That's just it, Em. I'm not happy."

A pause, then Emmy said, "I was wonderin' when you were going to realise it." She used the remote control to switch off the television. "Want to talk about it?"

"I just tried talking to Angel," Genevieve muttered abruptly.

"I imagine that didn't go too well. It's a damn shame the way your mother has been pressuring you to marry Colin."

Genevieve shook her white-gold head, her hair caught back in a single thickly braided rope. "Don't blame Angel, Em. I did it myself." Genevieve lifted her beautiful eyes. "What do you really think of Colin, Em?"

Put on the spot Emmy finally owned up. "I'm with Blaine," she said, not wishing to add she thought Colin Garrett nowhere near good enough for her darling Genni. Such a good girl. A lovely girl. Never given an ounce of trouble. Emmy would have found another position years ago only for Genni.

"Forget Blaine," Genevieve whispered, tears starting to her eyes. "He's been *awful* to me."

"But we can't forget Blaine, poppet," Emmy said. "Come on, admit it. You love him, hate him, whatever. He's always been there for you. Yet I have the feeling both of you are still only tapping into what you really mean to each other."

Genevieve inhaled a deep lungful of air. "He's a tyrant. Bloody-minded. He has too much power. Angel just told me he's paying for the wedding, I suppose the wedding dress, the bridesmaids' dresses, the flowers, the photographers, the church, the marquees, the mountains of food, the drink, the lot." She turned her violet eyes on Emmy, who knew a great deal more than she ever said.

"And that's upset you?"

"Upset me?" Genevieve nearly gave way to a primitive urge to scream. "It's devastated me. I wonder what else my mother *is* capable of? I suppose he's paid for everything for years." She bit her lip hard, realizing she was on the verge of crying.

"Blaine really cares about you, Genni," Emmy pointed out very gently. "He may be a little short with you from time to time but he's always had your best interests at heart."

"Isn't that nice! He frightens me," Genevieve suddenly admitted in a wobbly voice.

"Why, sweetheart?" Emmy, maternal by nature but childless, leaned forward, concern on her sunny-natured face.

Genevieve held her aching head. "He's maddening. He's a maddening man. And he has a cruel streak."

"No. I can't let that go," Emmy answered with an emphatic shake of her head.

"You always take his part, Emmy. Even *you.*"

"Because he's a fine man. I've been around you both a long time, Genni. I know how good Blaine has been to you."

Genevieve gave a miserable sigh, lost in the utter strangeness. She wanted Blaine so badly she was buckling under the strain. "So why has he turned against me, Em?"

"Why don't you ask him?" Emmy countered so vigorously she set her grey curls bouncing.

"What a joke." Genevieve hugged herself distractedly. "He's frozen me out, as you very well know."

Emmy nodded. "Something went very wrong that polo weekend."

Even remembering made Genevieve tremble the length of her. "It was just that… Oh, God, Em." She was drowning in the emotion that surfed through her blood. "Blaine was scathing when I told him I was going to marry Colin. He

didn't take me seriously enough. Then he flew into a cold
rage. Those glittering eyes! He told me we could never be
happy. He must have thought my education needed broaden-
ing because he pulled me to him so absolutely ruthlessly. I
thought he was about to beat me. Instead he kissed me, which
was *worse!* I heard stars burst."

Emmy swung her feet off the ottoman, looking at
Genevieve clutching her cheeks. "Kissed you? So he's kissed
you a million times."

"Oh, yes, throwaway kisses? Pecks on the cheek. Weren't
you listening, Em. I said *he kissed me.* Really kissed me. It
rocked me to my soul. It was brutal. It was brilliant. It was
horrible. I thought I was going to die."

"My goodness!" Emmy, knowing Blaine got the thrilling picture.

"There was *no* excuse for him," Genevieve said. "He did
it in such a way he's ruined my life."

"How's that, darlin'?" Emmy asked with a great rush of
protectiveness.

Genevieve looked back, startled. "Get real, Em. How can
I possibly marry Colin when Blaine kissed me? I'm afraid
of Blaine."

"That powerful?" Emmy looked at Genevieve with love
and understanding. She adored the girl.

"He's turned my world upside down, Em. Maybe he didn't
mean to. But he has. I was going along okay. But now! He's
pierced me like an arrow. So strange when he's planning on
getting married himself."

Emmy closed the box of chocolates carefully. "I take it you
mean Sally Fenwick?" she asked briskly.

"Of course I mean Sally." Genni didn't look up. "She's
lovely and kind. They've been very good friends for so long.
Sally is coming to the wedding. She's staying at the same
hotel. Even Hilary likes and approves of her." Genevieve

referred to Blaine's prickly young stepsister, several years younger than herself. "Hilary hinted marriage isn't far off."

"Really? I thought it was a bit of a one-sided relationship," said Emmy levelly.

"That's because Blaine never gives anything away."

"He kissed you. Some kiss by the sound of it."

Genevieve's face flared. "Blaine does everything like that, though, doesn't he? He doesn't realise he's so…"

"Powerful?" Emmy hit on the right word.

"God I hate him!" Genevieve said in a small voice.

"Why don't you tell him?" practical Emmy suggested.

"I did." Genevieve barely whispered it. "I told him I wanted him out of my life. I told him I was sick to death of his dictatorial ways. I haven't been able to do a thing to please him for years."

"Why don't you tell him *again?* You might get through this time."

Genevieve considered this, then shook her head. "I won't see him until he walks me up the aisle."

"So tell him tonight," Emmy pressed. "What's wrong with that?"

"You mean go to his hotel?"

Emmy nodded. "If I were you I'd do it like a shot."

Genevieve stared at her. "Emmy, darling, what are you saying?"

"Maybe what I should have said before. Tell Blaine what you tried to tell your mother. You can't go through with this marriage."

Genevieve sat erect in her chair and looked at her dear friend in alarm. "He'd be shocked out of his mind."

"I wonder," Emmy countered briskly.

"No Courtland would do such a terrible thing. Call off a wedding at the last moment."

"It's healthier than making a dreadful mistake, poppet."

Emmy leaned over to grasp Genevieve's arm. "Blaine's no ordinary man. Tell him what's in your heart. Let him take charge."

Genevieve's lovely face looked stricken. "I don't know if I dare. This is dreadful, Em. The house is ready. The church is ready. Our dresses are hanging upstairs. Fabulous dresses that cost a fortune. Three hundred guests are coming. The presents are all in. I don't know if I have the courage. I don't think I can humiliate Colin and his family. Colin's father might very well line up a pantechnicon to run me over. He's the Freight King after all."

"Listen, you've been bullied into this," Emmy snorted. "By Colin's steamroller of a father on the one hand and your conniving mother on the other. An engagement of a couple of months was diabolically clever. You haven't had time to know your own mind. But evidently Blaine's kissing you has changed it."

Genevieve's face mirrored her inner havoc. "I felt something I've never felt in my life. I felt Blaine owned me body and soul. That he's always been waiting for me to grow up. One kiss ended our old relationship. Dear God, I thought we were *family*. But it wasn't family in my blood. I can't deny I always thought he was the most marvellous man in the world, so exciting he makes the air vibrate, but we were cousins. I was his little Violetta. Remember how he used to call me that?"

"Oh, golly, I remember everything." Emmy's voice was low and wry. "Blaine has quite a way with words. For a very commanding man, daunting man at times, Blaine has his softer side. He could be very tender with you. Go to him, poppet. Pour out your heart. I have a feeling he'd pull down the stars for you if you asked him. No, don't look at me like that. It's true."

"It's not easy, Emmy," Genevieve said sadly. "I think Blaine wants our break to be permanent."

* * *

Hilary Courtland caught sight of Genevieve the minute she entered the hotel. Just seeing her gave Hilary a queer feeling when she'd been having a good time. Genevieve was moving with the speed and grace of a gazelle but Hilary got the impression of a deep unhappiness. Trouble, Hilary decided. Genni was looking for someone. Who else could it be but Blaine?

"Say, isn't that your cousin?" Hilary's male companion asked with immense interest. They'd been tucked away in a banquette, enjoying a mild flirtation, when he heard Hilary's odd little gasp and caught her startled gaze. Intrigued, he turned his head to follow up on the direction.

"Yes, that's Genevieve," Hilary answered, her smile twisted, her tone a lot more revealing than she intended. Ever since she could remember Hilary had felt rancour towards Genevieve. She was Blaine's sister yet Genni was the one Blaine had always cared about. Genni of the huge violet eyes and Rapunzel hair. Tonight Genevieve was casually dressed, navy gold-buttoned blazer, pale blue shirt, blue jeans, sneakers on her feet yet she looked like the model for the latest Ralph Lauren collection; a glamour girl like her dreadful femme fatale mother.

"God, she's a beauty, isn't she?" her companion commented, quite tactlessly. "Drop-dead gorgeous! How could a guy like Colin Garrett, even allowing for the Garret money, win *her* heart?"

"Well he has!" Hilary answered tartly, rendered almost dumb by jealousy. She put the lemon squash she was nursing down heavily and jumped to her feet. Genevieve appeared to be moving toward the bank of lifts. She had to stop her before she reached Blaine. She had to break what was coming up.

"Don't go away." She tossed a false smile at her boyfriend. "I'll have a word with her and I'll be right back."

Her companion waved her off. "Take your time." In actual fact he felt cheated out of meeting the gorgeous Genevieve.

What was she doing here alone this time of night? Whatever it was, it didn't suit Hilary. She looked upset. Perhaps trying to make sense of her cousin's unexpected appearance.

Hilary, a small pretty dark-haired, dark-eyed girl but without the Courtland stunning good looks and height, put on a burst of speed. She reached Genevieve just as she was about to step into a lift.

"Hey, Genni!" she called, using such an urgent tone people turned their heads.

"Hilary!" Genevieve turned about, doing her utmost to hide her dismay. For all her efforts to be friendly to Blaine's young stepsister she had long since realised Hilary would never like her. "What a surprise!"

"And where are you off to?" Hilary fixed Genevieve with big questioning eyes.

Genevieve felt most unwilling to confide in this moody girl but what excuse could she offer? "I wanted to see Blaine for a moment," she explained as casually as she could. "The receptionist said he was in."

"Actually he didn't go out." Hilary reached out confidentially for Genevieve's arm and drew her away. "He and Sally are making a night of it. They had dinner together in the hotel. He's with her now, if you know what I mean?" Hilary rolled her brown eyes expressively. "I'd leave whatever you wanted to ask him to the morning if I were you. You wouldn't want to embarrass them." She smiled her kitten smile.

God no! Genevieve felt pierced by an arrow, at that moment ready to flee.

"What is it, anyway? Maybe I can help you?" Hilary's voice had grown unabashedly affectionate as Genevieve's desperation slipped out.

"I don't think so, Hills."

"Try me." Hilary guided Genevieve to a couple of chairs. "You know you really will have to get over running to Blaine for help," she warned gently, unsuccessfully trying to keep her jealousy opaque. "This time tomorrow night you'll be a married woman." Hilary couldn't help herself. She smiled in broad triumph. "You'll be entering a new life. Your name will be Genevieve Garrett not Courtland. Isn't that thrilling?"

Quietly, Genevieve removed the other girl's small hand from her arm. She had never felt less thrilled in her life. "You've never liked me, have you, Hilary?" she said levelly, putting years of pretence to one side. "On this night of nights, please tell me. What have I ever done to you?"

Hilary burst into a cascade of tinkling laughter. "Oh, my, Genni, surely you know having you around changed my entire life. For the worse."

"In what way? Why on earth have you been afraid of me? I would never want to hurt you. We could have been friends. Good friends. We're cousins. We could have forged an unbreakable bond. But you would never let me get close."

"Why on earth would I when you had perfected the art of getting between me and my brother." Hilary's pretty face was set into unpleasant lines.

"You're talking nonsense, Hilary." Genevieve was feeling sicker by the moment. "It's so unfair. To me. To Blaine. He loves you."

"No, he doesn't. Not really. I don't touch his heart. What heart he has he reserved for you. The fatherless child." Hilary gave in to the huge temptation to say her piece. "Hell, you seduced him when you were a kid. You even robbed me of my father's love." A little sob rose to her throat. "When Dad was alive you used to twist him around your little finger. He hardly noticed me. I was the changeling in the Courtland fold."

Genevieve felt she might burst out crying, too.

"Hilary how did you let all this bitterness grow in your heart? It's *not true*. Not any of it. How long have you felt like this?"

"Since forever."

"Poor Hilary! You're breaking my heart," Genevieve said and meant it.

"I don't think so."

"Absolutely," Genevieve replied, feeling like she was mortally wounded.

"That's why I'm glad your getting married." Hilary smiled almost genially. "I knew one day you'd be out of our lives."

"That's no way to talk." Genevieve rose to her feet in protest. "How can you feel like this, say such things to my face, and still come to my wedding?"

"Why?" Hilary looked up at Genevieve, brilliant malice in her eyes.

"Because dear, sweet, beautiful, Genevieve, it's the day my brother will give you away forever."

Hilary was still sitting there feeling slightly shaky, but thrilled to have dispensed with the fleeing Genevieve, when Blaine suddenly materialised beside her, almost making her jump out of her skin.

"Isn't that Genni?" he demanded in the kind of voice that demanded a straight answer.

It took a tremendous effort for Hilary to pull herself together. How could she deny it? That white-gold rope of hair, the model figure, the grace of movement. "Yes, she just popped in to say hello." She tried a blithe smile, thinking fast.

"Damned odd." Blaine looked like he was about to take after her, such a restless radiance about him.

"Not really." Hilary rose, grasping her stepbrother's arm. "She and her bridesmaids were having a girl's night out. That was Genni's BMW parked out the front. Not supposed to do it, of course, but trust Genni to pull it off. A pity. You just missed her."

"And how was she?" Blaine bent his light lancing glance on his stepsister.

"Oh, lovely! Deliriously happy." Hilary turned an innocent face to him. "I've never seen a girl so much in love."

"The little fool!" Blaine's hard, handsome mouth tightened. "He'll never make her happy."

"But he *will,* Blaine," Hilary insisted, hugging her brother's arm. "She's the love of his life!"

And we're finally free of her.

"Don't," Blaine warned, his voice so strange Hilary stared at him vaguely terrified.

"Where's Sally?" she asked in an effort to divert him.

"She went home an hour ago." Blaine was still frowning, looking more formidable by the minute. "Surely you knew? We went right past you and your friend."

"I must have missed you," Hilary lied. "Sally's a darling. Mum and I are delighted she's the woman in your life."

"Don't be so dim-witted," Blaine responded impatiently, his eyes silver chips in his arresting dark face. "Your mother thinks no such thing. As for you? A bit of wishful thinking. Are you sure that's all Genni wanted?" he insisted. "To say hello?"

"What else?" Hilary wanted to turn and bolt, instead she lightly punched his shoulder. "She's on top of the world. I *am* family."

"So why did you turn down the role of bridesmaid?" Blaine challenged, giving her that lancing look that always made her feel so exposed.

She tried to make a joke of it. "You know. Genni's so tall. So are her friends. I didn't want to be the little pipsqueak in the middle. Genni understood. Come and join us for a minute." Hilary had a powerful nervous urge to draw her stepbrother away.

"No thanks." Blaine glanced down at her. "I want to leave a message at the desk. Goodnight, Hills. Sweet dreams."

She stood on tiptoe to kiss his lean cheek. "You, too, brother mine. It's going to be a wonderful day tomorrow. Like Genni, *I can't wait.*"

CHAPTER TWO

The Wedding Day

GENEVIEVE'S four bridesmaids, Tiffany, Montana, Penelope and Astrid, were scattered across her mother's enormous bedroom chattering and laughing, high on excitement, making minute adjustments to their bridesmaid gowns in a glorious palette of turquoise, fuchsia, lilac and violet, fanning out the voluminous silk skirts, tweaking the short sleeves that ballooned out from the ravishing off-the-shoulder necklines, smoothing the narrow tapered waistlines—all of the girls had been on a strict diet for a month: light breakfast on the day, absolutely nothing until the reception—settling their beautiful floral headpieces, works of art in themselves that matched the colour spectrum of their gowns. Each wore a necklace of twisted palest pink freshwater pearls with the clasp worn to the front, specially chosen to compliment their wonderful dresses—blue topaz, pink tourmaline, amethyst, sapphire— all set in an 18-carat-gold bezel, gifts from the bridegroom, Colin Garrett, heir to George Garrett, the Freight King.

"You should think about getting into your dress now, Genni," Angel urged, feeling a mite cross at her daughter's inappropriate lack of enthusiasm. "It's getting seriously late." She turned to waggle her fingers at the chief bridesmaid,

Tiffany, a statuesque honey-blonde, who walked into Angel's dressing room "the size of a department store with twice as much merchandise" as Tiffany had confided to her mother and emerged holding Genni's gown aloft.

"Here comes the bride," Tiffany tried to speak playfully but she, too, was perturbed by the look in her friend's eyes, so poignant it was painful to behold. It couldn't just be nerves. Genevieve looked very much like she didn't want to get married. Not to Colin Garrett anyway despite the fact many women including Tiffany herself found Colin very attractive.

"Wow!" Montana gave a mesmerized gasp as the others crowded around. "It's so beautiful it takes my breath away."

"Me, too!" Astrid agreed, visibly affected. Five times a bridesmaid, she was starting to feel like she was being passed over. But what a gorgeous creation was this gown! Thousands of seed pearls, tiny rhinestones and crystals glimmered on the tight-fitting off-the-shoulder ivory silk bodice, an exquisite pattern that was repeated around the hem of the beautiful billowing skirt.

"I can't wait to see you in it, Genni." Astrid, her shiny dark hair gathered into a deep upturned roll at the nape, looked towards her friend. "It's so absolutely you. I have to see you in it. Come on. You're so nervy you're turning me white."

Genevieve managed to laugh as she always laughed at her friend Astrid. "It seems to me I'm giving my life away."

Obediently she lifted her long slender legs exquisitely shod in handmade satin courts, stepping into her gown and standing perfectly still while her mother made short work of the long zipper in the back.

"Good God, Genni you've got terribly thin," Angel protested, giving an exasperated sigh. "The waistline could do with another tuck."

"It's all right," Genni insisted, edging away quietly. "Don't fuss, Angel. I want no fuss."

"All right, my darling. All right." Angel trilled, adopting a rare motherly tone to counteract Tiffany's look of veiled censure. Cheek of the girl! Someone should remind her of her manners. Angel continued to stare into her daughter's face, feeling a cold wave of panic.

Genevieve had tried to open her heart to her but she hadn't wanted to listen. *Still* didn't for that matter. She was so bloody desperate to get Genevieve married off to the right man. Someone who knew how to respect a beautiful mother-in-law and shower her with gifts. But under the silky golden tan she always had in summer Genni was very pale, her violet eyes so huge they dominated her small face. They seemed to be the only colour about her. Maybe her lipstick, in a luminous frosted rose, needed a heavier application, a touch more blusher? Angel concentrated hard.

"Now the veil!" Montana, the only one not feeling the tension or misinterpreting it as normal bridal jitters approached carrying the full-length tulle veil tenderly over her arm. The headpiece of three exquisite full-blown silk roses, pink and cream with touches of gold was already set in place. Genni was wearing her hair long and loose, the natural curl exaggerated by her hairdresser to suit the romantic conception.

"All right, sweetie?" Montana, very pretty with short caramel-coloured hair, looked at her friend carefully. A number of expressions flitted across Genevieve's face. Enough to suddenly make warning bells go off in Montana's head. Colin was very rich, a lot of fun, but admittedly he couldn't hold a candle to someone like…someone like…well, someone like Genevieve's cousin, for instance, Blaine Courtland, the big cattle baron. But he was *family,* the man who was giving Genevieve away. The man due to arrive in about ten minutes at the house.

"Genni's a bit stressed." Angel threw her daughter a bracing look. "Big weddings are always like this." Together she and Montana adjusted the full-length two-tiered tulle veil edged with the finest band of crystals.

"You look truly beautiful, Genni. You bring tears to my eyes." Montana very gently kissed her friend's cheek. "I wish you all the happiness in the world. One thing's certain, Colin will always make you laugh. If he hadn't fallen in love with you I'd have been after him myself."

"You were after him, darling," Astrid slipped in somewhat tartly.

Montana snorted in self-derision. "With Genni around I didn't stand a chance."

"Hold up your head, Genni!" clucked Angel, looking absolutely delicious not to say saucy in a light-as-air, sheer-as-silk aquamarine chiffon with swirls of gold and a colour-matched confection on her head that looked like some fabulous intergalactic butterfly had landed. "And do please try to smile."

Genevieve wasn't sure she could. Conflicting emotions were threatening to overthrow her and she was starting to feel stomach cramps. On one level she couldn't bear to be the cause of a dreadful scandal, the gossip columns would outdo each other in their efforts to blame her. Mention would be made of her notoriously fickle mother. She couldn't bear to bring pain and humiliation to the perennially light-hearted Colin. He trusted her. He wanted her. She wasn't absolutely sure he loved her. He certainly hadn't shown her an excess of passion. She knew that now.

He didn't like the way she was embroiled in the art scene, either. He gave no sign he was interested in her artistic talent, or indeed any artistic talent at all. She'd once dropped the name Jason Pollock into the conversation and Colin thought he was a property developer. His father, George Garrett, was certain to go ballistic. Even now she could hear his great booming voice in her ears, but George Garrett was the least of her worries.

She felt such a fool. Yes, fool was the right word. And one she had to live with. A fool nursing pure loss.

Blaine, as always, was right. She only wished to God he had never kissed her. Before that it had been so easy to hide from herself. Now she felt thoroughly exposed for what she was, a woman prepared to go through with a marriage because the groom had been extremely nice to her. Of course that could be attributed to the emotional deprivation of her childhood. How could she ever have imagined she was *in love* with Colin?

She was beginning to wonder if she even knew what love was. Overnight she'd turned into a different woman. She knew the why and when. That was when she should have found the courage to act instead of waiting until three hundred guests had put on their wedding finery and left for the church. She either had to go through with it to avoid a terrible mess or lock herself in her bedroom and refuse to come out. If only she could have spoken to Blaine last night. She had so desperately wanted to.

Weeping inwardly, she realised she had to summon up the strength to wipe Blaine from her mind. Blaine had his own life. His marriage to Sally was coming closer, as Hilary had confided. Genevieve just knew she couldn't bear to be around when that happened. Blaine was lost to her. The very thought got her moving. An action that had Angel muttering a short prayer of gratitude.

"Party time!" she cried. "I'm not sure if you're not the most beautiful bride I've ever seen in my life."

"Some people have all the luck," Astrid murmured in an aside to Tiffany, which wasn't exactly the most appropriate response.

"Well, let's get moving people." Angel clapped a little sharply. Exquisitely fashioned at a scant five-feet-nothing, Angel was nevertheless temperamental, demanding, something of a bully as Emmy could and did attest. "You look gorgeous, all of you," she cooed, revelling in her soon to be new status of adored mother-in-law. "One final inspection before you go out the door. I can't believe the big day has finally arrived."

Floating down the giant central marble staircase that would have done justice to Scarlett O'Hara, Tiffany wished she'd surrendered to an early desire to talk her friend out of this marriage. "Angel's euphoria doesn't appear to have worn off on Genn. She looks like she wants to do a runner," she whispered to Astrid, who by way of response grabbed Tiffany by her beautiful ballooning sleeve.

"Perfect! If Genn doesn't want to marry him he can marry me."

And there was worse to come. Downstairs Blaine Courtland had arrived. He stood in the marble-floored, flower-bedecked entrance hall, peonies, lilac branches, delphinium, roses, perfect carnations, looking upwards with eyes as brilliant as diamonds. He wore the traditional grey frock coat, grey trousers, waistcoat and a sapphire-blue satin cravat with a diamond stickpin, but his stunningly handsome face sported no smile. Indeed it appeared he, too, didn't feel like a wedding, although it was common knowledge on the grapevine he had paid for the whole thing.

"God, isn't he brilliant! The cattle baron," Montana muttered to Penelope. She was thrilled to be moving in such a world of wealth and glamour. "I'm mad about dark smouldering types with a cleft in their chins. Purple passion, you know." She gave Penelope a rather awful dig in the ribs.

"He's spoken for, darling," Penelope reminded her. "Sally Fenwick. Well-known pastoral family. Minor royalty."

"Wouldn't we all like to be," Montana groaned. "But shouldn't someone remind him it's a wedding we're going to. He looks a bit scary. *For-mi-dab-leh* as the French would say. I tell you, Tiff, there's something going on."

It was certainly starting to look like it. Genni didn't look happy. Neither did her cousin who exactly fitted the picture of the sort of man Genni should have married, Tiffany thought even as she recognised that simply wasn't on.

For as long as Tiffany had known Genni, coming up twelve years now, Genni had idolized her cousin, although of recent years Genni had confided he had hurt her badly by treating her as though she wasn't really capable of managing her own affairs. "He can be awfully rough on me!" Tiffany remembered Genni's exact words. This marriage had to be one of those times. Both young women in their conversations had made extravagant attempts to steer clear of any rapids. It was Angel who had engineered the whole wedding, Tiffany suddenly realised, making glorious lovers out of just good friends.

Her heart labouring in her chest, Genevieve hugged the polished railing as she made her way slowly down the staircase to the magnificent gallery-style entrance hall supported by massive marble columns. Angel was seriously into drama though to Genni's eyes there was always an over-abundance of everything.

But on this day of all days she didn't notice the artworks, the soaring fresco ceiling, breathtaking chandelier and grand golden console and mirror with so much ormulu it would have looked a whole lot better at Versailles. She only had eyes for Blaine. Loving him as she now found she did had to be her tragic secret. He looked magnificent but so stern-faced staring up at her, such a glitter to his eyes she felt like she was drowning in a silver lake.

Yet when she finally reached him, as though drawn by a powerful magnet, he bent his crown black head to kiss her cheek. "Hello, cherub," he murmured. "You look exquisite. I knew you would." His voice dropped lower, for her ears only. "I want to tell you, Genni, I'll always be here for you. No matter what happens. I'll never let anyone hurt you. Or make you unhappy."

She made a small sound of agony, her violet eyes burning in her pale face. "Oh, Blaine! Why couldn't I talk to you last night?" she implored.

Instantly his black brows drew together and his lean powerful body radiated a kind of menace. "You wanted to talk to me when you came to the hotel?" he questioned, his voice with an imperative note to it.

Electric tension seemed to be flashing all around them. It was in his face, in his remarkable eyes. She was afraid where it could lead. "It's all right, Blaine." Her voice vibrated a little wildly. "All right. It would have been too late anyway."

"What?" He grasped her two hands and took them firmly in his own. "I need to know what you mean, Genni? Don't be afraid."

But I am afraid, she thought passionately. Afraid of you and what you mean to me. Afraid of my own feelings that have grown and grown like some monstrous secret flower.

"All right there, Blaine, Genni?" Angel who had been concentrating on fastening the clasp of her diamond bracelet that matched the sunburst on her shoulder now called, shooting anxious eyes at them. She had always been aware on some deep unprobed level Blaine and her daughter shared an unbreakable bond.

Blaine ignored her, his entire attention focused on Genni. "Genni, you've got to tell me the truth." His voice was low and taut. "Do you love this man?"

There was a moment of rushing silence. It was now or never. Then she remembered Sally. Sally at this year's celebratory Polo Ball with Blaine's gorgeous orchid pinned to her evening dress. Sally beaming with pride as people turned to see her and Blaine together. Sally looking for Blaine the moment he moved out of sight, eyes moving rapidly around the room. Sally hugging his arm.

"I must do, Blaine," Genni answered quietly. "I'm going to marry him."

"This is something you really want?" Clearly he still didn't believe her.

"God, Blaine, you're so unrelenting." Wanting to punish him as he had punished her, she spoke fiercely, in so much pain, so much pride, it was important she stop him from questioning her further. It was all too late. Colin had pursued and won her. Not Blaine. No matter what, Blaine was lost to her.

"I'm sorry." He dropped her hands at once, his dark high-mettled face now closed against her. "Forgive me. I wish you all the happiness in the world."

"I know you don't," Genni found herself responding wildly, too far gone to care. They were almost on the verge of one of their monumental arguments.

"Be careful what you say," Blaine warned, his eyes narrowed to mere slits.

In the entrance hall everyone stood around absolutely enthralled by what was going on between Genni and her commanding cousin. Although no one could make out what was being said, the body language told them heaps. There was grief, anger, and hurt, a raging that looked like antagonism. Genni's face was still very white but a high colour burned her cheeks. From stillness she had burst into abandoned brilliant life.

It wasn't looking good. Angel had the dismal feeling the two of them might just up and away. On the point of desperation, concerned for their every move, Angel stepped in. "Photographs people!" She turned swiftly to snap her fingers at the society photographer, Bernard, famous for his designer weddings, who gave no indication whatsoever he saw or heard her. "Then we really should be leaving for the church."

"There's time, Angelica." Blaine glanced briefly at his watch feeling like a lion wanting to protect its young. No one was going to *push* Genni into marriage. "Anyway, isn't it fashionable to be late?"

It was unless one had a great deal of worry on one's mind. Blaine was a man capable of anything, Angel thought, hustling them all into the spectacular formal living room with its breathtaking views of Sydney Harbour.

"You're over here, Blaine, next to me," she cooed, hoping to God Blaine would calm down.

Such was the severity of Blaine Courtland's expression everyone was amazed when he actually crossed the floor to tower over the petite Angel, five-three, and she was wearing high heels.

"I don't like the way Genni is acting," he told Angel, staring across the room at her. "If she's not entirely happy about this marriage, there's still time to bail out."

Just when Angel had a horror Genni was about to do just that. "Blaine, darling, you can't be *serious?*" A superb actress, she sounded amazed. "Every single day Genni has been telling me how happy she is. How much she loves Colin. They were made for each other. Soul mates!"

"Rubbish!" Blaine corrected very bluntly. "When you're madly in love with someone you don't look like Genni does now. I know her too well."

"But goodness, darling, you've never *been* madly in love with anyone, so how would you know?"

"Simple. You really should take time off to try and understand your daughter. Anyway, any woman I've been involved with is still my friend, which is a damned sight more than you can say of your two husbands and assortment of gigolos."

"You loved saying that, didn't you, darling?" Angel, unfazed by the hard truth, pulled a little face. "Sometimes, Blaine, you can be absolutely dreadful."

"When Genni's happiness and well-being is put on the line, yes," he acknowledged brusquely. "Look at her, Angel.

Forget yourself and your plans. Look at Genni. She's as white
as a snowdrop." His glittering grey gaze was directed to the
centre of the overly grand room where Genni was being posed
by Bernard in front of the white marble fireplace. It was
adorned with a great abundance of white roses and green
tracery topped and outdone by a large portrait of Angel in a
deliciously low-cut blue-satin ballgown painted during the
halcyon days of her ill-fated first marriage.

"God, I don't believe this," Blaine muttered blaming himself
for not simply kidnapping the bride. A hundred vivid memories
of Genevieve flitted through his head. The adorable two-year-
old with her radiant violet eyes and riot of platinum curls.

He'd been ten years old when his father's favourite cousin,
Stephen, had brought his little daughter to Jubilee. A difficult
ten-year-old, hard to handle. A boy who already knew despair
because his beautiful mother had abandoned him and his father
and run off with her lover. An event so unexpected, so out of
character, he sometimes thought he was still in a state of shock.

Genni had come into his life at the right time. Over the
years he had given her all the love his heart could hold. She
was so innocent, so vulnerable, so sweet-sassy intelligent, so
generous with her affections.

As Stephen and Angel drifted further and further apart
Genni had come to spend more time at Jubilee where she was
back with her "cherished" Blaine. How close they had been
then. It seemed he had taught her everything. How to swim,
how to ride, how to handle a gun, how to find her way around
the bush, how to survive. What he hadn't been able to teach
her was how to pick the right men. In fact from about seven-
teen he'd been in despair about Genni's choices. Not a one
good enough for her.

Certainly not Garrett, though loaded with money and a
certain easy charm, he was short on substance. The more he
had tried to tighten his hold on her, the more Genni had flown

into little wild rages, claiming where he had once loved her now she was always in high disfavour. It wasn't true. He was hungry in spirit for the old easy relationship, but over the past few years an odd constraint had grown between them neither of them seemed to know how to break. Genni no longer ran to him for advice and comfort. Or did she? What was she doing at the hotel last night? Hilary had told him Genni had paid the visit to her. He should have known better about his stepsister's wiles. The unfortunate truth was Hilary had a deep-seated jealousy of Genevieve. Everyone in the family knew it, just as they knew Hilary had grown into her own worst enemy.

While Blaine brooded, his eyes like jewels, Angel was saying quite merrily, "Genni looks perfectly happy to me, darling. A touch of bridal jitters, no more." She reached up to pat Blaine's lean tanned cheek. "You're worrying about nothing," she said softly. "You always did have a powerful urge to keep Genni to yourself." Angel smiled as she watched Bernard straighten Genni's long beautiful veil. "Isn't her bouquet fabulous?" She smiled proudly. "You can't beat Hughie Rickman for flowers."

Blaine answered with such terseness it could easily have been interpreted as profound disapproval. "She's the most beautiful thing I've ever seen, but no one, not even Genni herself, can convince me she's in love with this guy. I can't have her marrying a man she doesn't love."

At the sweep-all-before it note in his voice, Angel put a trembling hand to her breast. Only for her deep concern for her makeup she would have been in tears. "Blaine, maybe you've got a problem," she suggested. "Genni hasn't." She lifted her face to him, despite herself pierced through with his wondrous blue-blooded aura. "You can't always run her life. You're here to give her away, my dear. In under a half hour you and Genni are going to do the grand march down to the altar. I know both your lives will change, but look on the bright side. You won't have to worry about her any more. You won't have to pick up all the bills." She said it totally without embarrassment, but Blaine answered with the merest lick of contempt.

"We're not talking about money. Everything would be fine if only I could believe Genni is marrying the man she loves."

His radar was working too well. "Blaine, darling," Angel tried her most convincing voice, tilting back her head so she could look him directly in the eye. "My daughter told me only last night never in her life has she been so happy." Telling fibs was one of Angel's lifelong specialities. "And she'll never want for anything, isn't that wonderful?"

Apparently that didn't thrill Blaine at all. "Who the hell cares about that?" he retorted in a low burned-up voice. "She couldn't be stupid enough to marry just for money?"

Angel was amazed by such a view. "That's all very well for people who have tons of it," she responded. "Money is way too good to pass up."

Blaine gave a weary sigh. "I just hope your outlook hasn't rubbed off on Genni," Blaine responded tautly. "There's much too much to her for the likes of Garrett. I liked him well enough when Genni first brought him to Jubilee but I never thought for one minute he was the man she was seriously considering marrying."

It was hard indeed to sound nonchalant. "Go on, darling," Angel teased. "I'm sure Genni tried to tell you. I know you really care about her but you don't show her much tenderness. The truth is your father's daunting manner spilled over on you. Genni fell head over heels in love with Colin. The only person who *didn't* know about it was you." Angel gave her tinkling laugh that held quite an edge.

It was Bernard the society photographer who halted Blaine's searing retort. "Pardon me?" Bernard called, struggling with his own radar. "It's your turn now, mother of the bride." He bowed gracefully in Angel's direction, though he hadn't taken to her one bit, "and the bride's very distinguished cousin, the well-known cattle baron, Mr. Blaine Courtland. I can't let *you* get away."

"God!" Blaine muttered beneath his breath, feeling Angel's small hand sneak into his as though he was too, too dear to her. In a few minutes he would have Genni alone in the car. He would be as gentle as he knew how with her. Angel's reference to his "lack of tenderness" had really stung. It was deserved. He was desperate now to get Genni to reveal her heart. He knew precisely how *he* felt. Every atom of his being was steeled against giving her away. If his instincts were correct beneath that exquisite bridal exterior Genni was screaming for help.

Inside the stretch limousine Genni sat very quietly in all her wedding finery, the billowing silk skirt stretched out over the seat, her veil arranged to one side lying in a foaming cloud atop it, looking determinedly out the window. If she dared to chance a look at Blaine sitting opposite her, he would recognise her despair. Even now she was fighting hard to keep the tears from welling into her eyes.

"Blaine," she said soundlessly over and over, trying to draw strength from just his name "I love you. I'll always love you." The knowledge was like a physical blow to the heart. Without food—she hadn't been able to eat a bite of breakfast—she felt dizzy and disoriented, caught up in a scenario Angel might well have written. I can't do this to myself. I can't do this to Colin, Genni agonised. He mightn't adore the ground I walk on but he deserves better than a wife who doesn't love him.

She started violently when Blaine suddenly reached over and caught her hand. "God, Genni. You'd think you were a winter bride. Your hands are freezing." He began to rub them, warming them in no time because her blood caught fire. "Angel took me to task back at the house. She told me a truth about myself I had to hear. I haven't been terribly kind to you of late, have I? As your mother put it, I haven't shown you much tenderness."

The admission nearly annihilated her. There was such a sparkle of tears behind her eyelids. "I haven't been very nice, either," she whispered. "The strange thing is, I don't have a temper with anyone else but you. You make me fly apart."

"That much, cherub, is obvious," he said dryly. "I know I'm too high-handed, too dismissive of what seems to me frivolous stuff. You have to make allowances for me. The thing is, Genni, I'm committed to something really important. *Your happiness.* No, don't shrink away from me," he begged as she leaned back and shut her eyes so aware of him she felt he was invading her. Body and soul. "I know you, Genni. I used to know you, anyway," he added wryly, with that irresistible sparkle in his beautiful eyes she so loved. "Just tell me once more—the last time, I promise—tell me you love Colin. That your dearest wish is to marry him?"

Such was her emotional state Genni had difficulty remembering Colin's face. "Please, Blaine, can you stop asking me?"

"No." He shook his dark head. "If you're frightened you must go through with this, just tell me. I'll take care of everything," he told her with that hard masculine authority. "It'll be a nine-day wonder but there will be life after."

Will there? Genni's thoughts went back to Sally Fenwick. "Hilary told me you and Sally are coming around to setting your own wedding date?" Once more she averted her head, looking sightlessly out the window.

Blaine turned her head back to him, loving and hating the sight of her in her glorious wedding dress. "Is that what Hilary said to you last night?" he demanded, his tanned skin lit by anger.

"She might have." Genni, too, was flushed; upset enough to jump out of the car. "Please, Blaine, don't torment me. It would mean everything to me if you could respect how I feel."

"When your heart is racing? When I can gauge what you feel through my palm?" His laugh was low and savage. "If it weren't so goddam lunatic I'd believe you're trying to get back at me for kissing you. There's no one, but *no one* like you for doing that."

"Then why *did* you?" Her breath trembled in her throat. "It shocked me so much I nearly fainted."

"I remember," he reminded her bitterly. "I was there."

"*Why,* Blaine?" She stared at him with her violet eyes, the urge to know consuming her. "You changed everything in a few moments." The power and the cruelty of the man!

"Did I?" He put his hands to either side of her, making her a prisoner. "You think about that, Genni. With my mouth on yours it didn't feel like you didn't want it."

Overwhelmed, she looked down. "And you betrayed Sally!"

He made a sound of complete exasperation. "Don't be so damned silly. Sally is a friend. A good friend, but she's not a woman I'd dream about. I've never cared about anyone like I care about you."

"Yes, as your little pet. Not a grown-up *woman.*"

"We're not back to that again, are we?"

He drew away from her, his luminous eyes pure silver.

"Not *ever.* You've got some idea I can't live without you. But I've got news for you." Her words shrilled and trembled so, she was grateful for the glass panel that separated them from the chauffeur. "*I'm going to marry Colin.*" Even as she said it she despised herself.

"And make a mess of your life?"

"You're so nasty, so…caustic…"

"Sad to say I am, just as you're so provocative. You know the dark depths in me, Genevieve. You're as used to my outbursts as I am to yours. I don't know about the chauffeur, if he can hear us. I haven't handled you particularly well of recent times. For that I genuinely apologise. It has all come out so badly because I couldn't seem to reach you. You were dead set on defying me at every turn. In fact you gave me hell."

There was truth at the heart of it. She could see it clearly now. "Don't. I love you," she admitted passionately. "I'm sorry. I'm sorry. Am I making any sense at all?"

"I'm afraid not." His answer was crisp. "You're not happy. That's obvious. You need a man who can set you alight. Do you think I haven't seen you incandescent? Women are such strange creatures. I'll never understand them." He said it like it might have been a curse.

Forlornly, Genevieve touched the exquisitely decorated bodice of her wedding gown. "Why did you never tell me you were paying for all this?"

He closed his eyes against the surge of hot anger. "I wish to God your mother could keep her mouth shut."

"I feel seared by shame."

"How ridiculous!" He sounded thoroughly stirred up. "You're family." God, that's *wrong*. For a moment he couldn't speak. Then as he glanced out the window he was shocked to see they had arrived at the church. Media photographers were in attendance, standing slightly apart from the crowd of on-lookers that had gathered to see a bride well known to them through the social pages.

The bronze-polished skin on Blaine's face was stretched taut. "I'm not the kindest person in the world, Genni, but I'm here for you." His expression suggested only one word. *Action.* "Unless you're going happily into this, it would be better, far better, to stop it now."

For a moment hope glimmered, then she heard the oohs and aahs of the crowd. "For God's sake, Blaine, I'd be a social outcast. Help me to go through with it."

"Are you crazy?" He could crush her to him with one arm. Drag her away.

"Yes." She was finished and she knew it. Her mind reeled as the chauffeur came round to open her door. She could see her old life slide by. People were moving closer, waving and smiling, the photographers already shooting their pictures.

Please God help me, she prayed devoutly. Help me out before it's too late. I know I deserve this but I truly didn't understand my own heart.

That same heart bursting, Genevieve found herself standing out on the footpath to much applause while the designer of her gown fussed around her, settling her billowing silk skirt, adjusting her long froth of a veil.

"Isn't she beautiful!" came time and again from the crowd, but Genni didn't register the compliments. She felt she had the weight of the world on her shoulders instead of her wedding veil.

"Well?" Blaine gave her his arm, hovering over her inches over six feet, devastatingly handsome, the man who was to give her away, but the expression in his shimmering eyes was anything but family.

I'll love you always. Had she spoken it or thought it?

Only she had not known, had not understood that love at all.

What was going on here? Warren Maitland, the dress designer, thought in amazement. He simply couldn't *imagine* but his gown, his creation was gorgeous. So was the bride who looked like she mistook the cousin, the man who was to give her away, for the bridegroom. Maitland didn't believe any girl could look at a man like that and not be madly in love with him. In that moment, a trained observer, he sensed major scandal looming.

As if under a spell Genni found herself walking into the wonderfully picturesque old church, leaning into Blaine and on his arm. Where their flesh touched, it *burned.* It all had the

quality of a dream to her. She could hear the music, the
emotive swell of the organ; she could see her bridesmaids just
inside the church. The elegantly dressed guests seated in the
pews, so *many* of them, some had jetted in from overseas. Oh,
God, for what? The pews were decorated with white satin
ribbons. The altar luminous with white roses. Colin was
waiting up there. Colin and his friends. She breathed and
breathed, but she couldn't get enough air. She was going
away…fainting…in front of her eyes a field of stars. The last
thing she heard was Blaine saying her name…

If Genni hadn't solved the dilemma herself Blaine would
have simply scooped her up, locked her to him, to face the
Furies. The wretchedness in her had been transmitted by the
curled-up fingers on his arm. He felt her response in every
nerve. It had pierced him through the heart.

What was done was done, he thought. He moved with in-
credible swiftness to gather the swooning bride up into his
arms, her beautiful veil floating like a cloud above the waves
of breezes that blew in the Gothic doorway. With high relief
he saw his cousin Marc, a medical man, rush down the aisle to
Genni's aid, the bridesmaids parting like fields of flowers at
his approach. They weren't going to wait until Genni came out
of this faint, Blaine vowed. They were going home. And by
home he meant Jubilee. He would kidnap Genni if he had to.

While Blaine waited for them a tall powerful figure, with
Genni light as thistledown in his arms, long silk skirt cascading to the floor, they came.

Angel first, looking all of a sudden, years older. Colin, the
bridegroom, followed by his best man, both looking utterly
bewildered as if they didn't understand what was going on.
The bridegroom's parents, George and Victoria Garrett,
George huffing and puffing, shaking his bald head in disbelief, the mother looking like she was going to ask for the engagement ring back. Some of the guests collapsing against

one another murmuring who knows what? Some looking helplessly over their shoulders as if the person behind them could explain exactly what was happening; some full of concern and sympathy, others cynically pondering the possible reason for the faint. The bridesmaids darted desperate looks at one another. Genevieve gradually came to, knowing on this day at least she wasn't about to say, "I do!"

On doctor's orders the ceremony was "postponed." Doctor Marc Courtland, trapped by the fiercely commanding look in his cousin Blaine's eyes, shook his head ruefully. "Nervous exhaustion" was the diagnosis. The bride obviously needed complete rest.

No one could stop the flood of speculation. With so many guests all dressed up with nowhere to go, it was decided at least the food and drink had to be consumed. With Genevieve tucked away in a very private room in a very expensive private hospital. Angel who had always lived in an operatic lifestyle invited everyone who wished to come back to the house to do so. An astonishing number of people took advantage of her hospitality, desperate to talk about it all—someone must have some dramatic revelations to divulge—and see inside Angel's mansion, which was said to be pretty extravagant.

The Garretts, not surprisingly, disappeared into the night, George Garrett looking very much like the deal was off, while most of the guests pressed ahead famished for food and gossip.

The groom, after he returned from a brief visit to the hospital where he was allowed only a few words with his paper-white would-be bride, was later seen dancing with one of the bridesmaids, apparently not worried about the cataclysmic events of the afternoon or what certain people had plunged into whispering like some soap opera: the bride was really in love with her cousin, Blaine Courtland, the man who was supposed to have given her away. The extraordinary thing was, no one seemed to condemn him. In fact everyone, including the bridegroom, appeared to think him the better man.

If that were true, and at least twenty or more guests, including the bride's mother and the head bridesmaid didn't register amazement, how had it all come to pass? Love was such a force, what complexities of life had brought Genevieve and Blaine to that point?

To understand one would have to go back....

CHAPTER THREE

The Lead-Up

IT HAD been a wonderful day all 'round. A day of high heat
and shimmering mirage, capped off by a late afternoon dust
storm that blew in from the desert, covering them all with billowing clouds of red dust.

Midmorning one of the mustering crew had come off his
motorbike, broken a leg and cracked a few ribs. Soon after,
he got the perturbing news the new jackeroo, a kid called
Marshall, had been bitten by a desert taipan in the gidgee
scrub out at Camp Moggill. No accident, the kid had been fool
enough to pick the snake up. Showing off.

God! He could scarcely believe it. And the bloody thing
had hung on, its fangs embedded in the boy's arm. He'd had
to dash the snake's brains out before he could administer
what the station had left of the antivenene. Just a couple of
life-saving vials. At that time the kid was barely conscious,
muttering over and over he was a total drongo. He couldn't
disagree with that.

He'd got off an emergency call to the Flying Doctor post-
haste, getting both victims to the station airstrip while they
waited for the Super King Air to fly in. Bob Carlin, a great
bloke and a fine doctor, had given the boy another shot to be

on the safe side. Clarry's leg they'd already set in splints but it needed to be X-rayed.

What might be called a true-blue day. He was desperate for a bath and an ice-cold beer. He could almost feel the tingle in his mouth; nevertheless he worked on tirelessly, not arriving back at the homestead until well after a burning red sun had gone down so slowly it might have been stuck in the sky. A sure sign they'd have more of the same tomorrow.

He entered the house through the back way, not wanting to scatter red dust as he went. The light was on in Lally's room so he made his way down the rear hallway to say hello. Lally was his maiden aunt, Eulalia Courtland, his father's sister. She had come to them after his mother had run off, staying on until his father rebounded into another marriage less than two years later. After his father's funeral he had invited Lally to return to her former home, an invitation she had accepted with tears in her eyes, and Lally wasn't a woman who cried easily. She had been very good to him. He wasn't a man who forgot. Then, too, Lally unlike his stepmother, Delia, and his stepsister, Hilary, shared his powerful love for the land and the remote cattle station that was the Courtlands' ancestral home. Lally was an Outback person. As was he. As was….

Genni.

For a moment his mouth softened unbelievably despite his current turbulent mood towards her. Old memories returned. Genni. The cutest little kid with all the charm in the world. How in the world had she turned into such a blazing hellcat ready to defy him at every turn? Their wonderful relationship based on mutual loyalty and affection, a wealth of shared interests, had almost overnight turned so tempestuous they spent most of their time goading each other. He was supposed to be tough, not a man to cross, most people painted him that way, yet one slip of a girl could and did continually throw him off balance.

Damn her and her silly romances. The last guy she brought out to the station most likely to irritate him, didn't even know how to saddle up a horse. Genni and her boyfriends! Genni and her dreadful mother, the scatty egocentric Angelica, known as Angel. What a misnomer! All of the family to a man blamed Angel for the tragic early death of her first husband, Stephen Courtland, Genni's father and his own father's favourite cousin though one had been a cattle man and the other had followed his dream of becoming an architect. The dream hadn't lasted long.

"Uncle Steve," a courtesy title, had been just as bad a picker of women as his own father. Both women had brought chaos into their husbands' lives. Both had borne their husbands a child. Him and Genni. At least Angel, retaining custody of Genni, had stuck around. His own mother, Crystelle, had run away and never come back. Boy, oh boy, some mother.

At ten he'd had to learn overnight how to stand on his own two feet. He'd had to learn how to cope with heartbreak. *In silence.* His father hadn't helped him. From the day Crystelle left his father he had cut her out of their lives. Her name was never mentioned.

Not even Lally had dared to go against his father's orders, and Lally was a strong personality in her own right. Though she didn't know much about children, with few inbuilt maternal skills, Lally had tried. He was closer to her—the Courtland blood—than he had ever been to Delia who, too, had tried to win his boyish affection but failed. He blamed himself. After his mother's desertion he couldn't seem to open his heart to any strange women. Lally was family. She spoke his language. Delia, pretty, softly spoken, kindly and well meaning as she was to this day, he'd regarded and treated as a stranger for many years. He regretted his cruelty. Delia didn't deserve it. These days they had an easy relationship with little or no friction. It was Genni who had started the thaw on his heart imbuing in him the faith in life destroyed by his mother.

The unforgettable Genni, the little…bitch, he fumed. She certainly had a major talent for exposing his temper.

"Land sakes, you look like a Red Indian!" Lally greeted him, looking up from her book.

"So would you be if you were out in all that dust." He flashed her a very white smile out of a darkly tanned dust-covered face.

"And how's the boy?" There was concern on Lally's handsome regal face.

"He's learned a powerful lesson. Bob thinks he'll be okay. Clarry went off like the stoic he is."

Lally nodded her agreement, turning away for a moment to pick up a letter from her open bureau. "There's mail for you. Came in on the freight plane."

"I won't read it now." Blaine made to move off. "Just wanted to say hello. I badly need a good scrub. Who's it from, anyway?"

Lally's mouth pursed. "Jinx, would you believe!"

"Probably a sweetly worded request for more money." His grin was cynical.

"I suppose so." Lally gave a deep sigh. "Angel's devotion to money is complete. She's outrageous. Trades on your love for Genni."

He shrugged. "Tell me about it. The only thing is, Genni is not in my good books of late."

Lally reacted swiftly. "Come off it! You're still her hero."

He stared away across the room, his expression regretful. "I was until a few years ago then she got as sassy as all hell."

"Girls, too, like their independence, my boy," Lally reminded him, tucking her glasses into the pocket of her shirt.

"I can't seem to deal with it," he admitted wryly.

His aunt watched him closely. "Well *I* think you're won-derful. Of course, I'm biased, but you're not *perfect*. You've become a bit phobic about Genni, dear. Trying to protect her from everything. She has to learn."

"Not from her mother." Concern soared again in him. "Angel is a bad influence. You've said that yourself. I'd just hate to see Genni follow in Angel's footsteps."

"Well, here now." Lally sat up straight in her armchair, shaking her silver-grey head vigorously. "Genni is *our* side of the family. She's a far more intelligent, more sensitive and generous person than Angelica could ever be. Angel really only lives for herself."

"I know that," Blaine said, looking a mite dispirited, "but Angel encourages Genni to mix with the wrong people. She has the wrong expectations for her. Hell, Genni wouldn't have gone to university only for me. Angel was going to pack her off to New York, launch her into the modelling world."

"That wouldn't have happened, Blaine," Lally soothed. "Genni didn't want it despite her mother's all-out campaign. In many ways Angel is unstoppable. But Genni has her father's artistic nature. I believe she'll make a fine painter one day."

"I agree. She's pretty damned good now." Blaine exhaled an impatient sigh. "Genni should be concentrating on that aspect of her life instead of running around with a string of lightweight boyfriends. God, I'm really worried Angel will try to marry her off to some rich moron. After all, money is the only thing that counts with Angel."

"Indeed it is. She's obsessed with it, as we know. But there's one important difference, my dear. Money is not the most important thing in the world to Genni. She'll never marry a man she doesn't love."

"Marry?" For a moment Blaine slumped heavily against the doorjamb, rangy body suddenly showing signs of weariness. "Genni needs a lot more living, a lot more maturity before she decides to take on a husband. Hell, the very idea!" He sounded outraged.

"At least you're taking picking the right mate very seriously," Lally said slyly.

He looked at her lazily, then gave her his beautiful smile, a smile that was impossible to resist. "*Don't*, Lally! The thought of marriage brings on a major depression. Who would put up with me?"

Lally snapped her fingers. "Any young woman you asked. You're almost shockingly handsome. You have a fine respected name. You're a dynamo like your father. It has to be said you're not nice and sweet all the time, especially around Genni, but you sure pack an aura."

He straightened from the doorway immediately. "Catch you next time!"

"I'm not saying I object to your lack of vanity," Lally called after him. "Go on, have your bath. Angel's letter will keep."

He finally got 'round to reading it before he went down to dinner. Just Lally and him. Delia and Hilary were having one of their many holidays away, this time in Indonesia, Central Java, to visit the ninth-century Buddhist stupa of Borobudar, the largest Buddhist monument in the world.

"A spiritual journey to enlightenment," Hilary had called it. He hoped it would have some effect on her. His young stepsister, spoiled and overindulged in many respects by her mother, had some kind of inner vulnerability that forever made her feel unloved and insecure.

Ever since he could remember, Hilary had always been in jealous competition. First for their father's love, then when their father had died three years back after suffering a terrible spinal injury out on muster, Hilary had turned her attentions to him. Whenever Genevieve had come to visit there had always been lots of screaming and yelling from Hilary as her somewhat morbid fixations became more intense. The two girls could have been friends. Genni certainly tried. Even Hilary had to acknowledge that, but they never did get on. The reason was obvious to everyone. Hilary had to be first in her father's then her brother's affections so anyone else she perceived got in the way was viewed with antipathy and resentment.

Delia who had done practically everything in her power to remedy matters before turning to over-compensating, always insisted Hilary would grow out of it. So far Hilary hadn't, and she was going on nineteen. No great age, he realized, too, which was what made him so patient with her and he wasn't patient by nature, what Hilary believed was actually *true*.

Both he and his father had treated Genni as though she was more a part of them than their own flesh and blood. But Genni had made it so easy. Herself deprived of her much loved father with a mother who always put herself first, Genni had never vyed for attention, emotionally or any other way. Naturally sunny-natured, known for her childhood adoration of him, such things had made friendship between the two girls impossible. One day when Hilary was happily married with a family of her own—his fondest wish come true—he hoped she would leave all her insecurities behind. Meanwhile Hilary had a real talent for causing problems.

At least he got the reason for Angel's letter right. As usual she was after a loan—he had no record of her ever repaying anything—she didn't know where her money went—unless it was keeping herself and Genni well dressed. Angel wasn't close to a con woman, he thought darkly. She was. He knew for a fact Angel rarely bought Genni anything. Genni from the first week she started work had paid her own way. He'd certainly bought Genni a car for her seventeenth then her twenty-first birthday, the BMW she looked after like a baby. Jewellery from time to time, seeing Angel couldn't be persuaded to part with any of hers.

Angel, meanwhile in between husbands, sent along all the bills she couldn't handle. Most he paid. Ones in connection with the house, maintenance, rates, improvements—after all, Genni lived at home—some he knocked back, antique dealers in particular. They had to see Angel coming. Jubilee homestead was considered rather grand but it paled in comparison to Angel's over the top mansion paid for with Courtland money.

At the bottom of the letter by way of a P.S. would Blaine "darling" mind if she brought her current beau, a guy called Slocombe to the annual Polo Ball, this year to be hosted by Jubilee. He had no objection so long as Genni tagged along.

Maybe it would be one of those nights when there was a blissful lack of tension between them. One when Genni would show less provocation and he more tolerance. He had never got to the point when he had seriously considered turning her over his knee, but…! For someone who looked like she did, she had unearthed all manner of turbulent emotions in him. Some he kept tightly canned as though even thinking them was unforgivable. Genni was family! The adorable little girl child with the big violet eyes, white-gold ringlets. The bright star in his life. The prospect of losing sight of that thoroughly unnerved him.

Delia and Hilary arrived home at the end of the following week, physically tired but full of the wonders of their pilgrimage. Indeed Hilary was so inspired she went so far as to announce to a family—who wanted for nothing more—she had achieved "a purer higher state of mind." A claim almost immediately knocked out of the water when Lally told them over a specially prepared delicious three-course dinner, Genni and her mother, as well as her mother's current boyfriend, would be coming to the Polo Ball, which was only a fortnight off.

Hilary exhaled sharply, a gasp of classic outrage. The peaceful expression on her pretty, golden-skinned face was instantly transformed into the sort of storminess that had nearly defeated them all. "The story of my life," she cried hotly, knife and fork frozen in midair. "I get myself a fabulous new dress,

I watch my diet the whole time we're away just so I can fit into it, and Genni has to turn up to outshine us all. I really shouldn't have bothered." Now she banged the silverware down.

Blaine, who had had a very hard day, even allowing for his extraordinary recuperative powers, was fed up. "That'll do," he said crisply. "Seems to me you haven't changed a great deal, despite the grand trek. When are you going to give up this tiresome jealousy of Genni? We're all getting sick and tired of trying to humour you. You're your own person with your own special qualities. You must see a pretty girl when you look in the mirror. The way you carry on anyone would think you were downright ugly."

"I swear I am," Hilary burst out, her dark eyes flashing dramatically.

Delia, sitting opposite her, sought as always to appease the daughter who was beginning to quite intimidate her. "No, no, darling," she smiled comfortingly, "you're really lovely. You *are.* Your dress is so beautiful you're going to look ravishing."

"I'm not," Hilary said even more gruffly, sweeping her short glossy brown bangs from her forehead. "Genni makes a positive practice of putting me in the shade."

Lally who didn't interfere often was driven to speak up.

"Genni does no such thing!" she said emphatically in her well-bred voice.

"The new woman!" Blaine saluted his stepsister ironically.

High colour mottled Hilary's cheeks as she flashed Lally a glance like a small poison dart. "All I'm saying is can't Genni stay home for once? And that batty Angel? Every time she opens her mouth I want to strangle her. And her boyfriend. I bet he's horrible. Filthy rich and terrible vulgar. Why don't they just stay away for once?"

"Because I invited them," Blaine responded, quite patiently for him. "If you weren't such a grouch you'd notice Angel adds quite a lot of sparkle to these occasions. Every head turns when she walks in the door. She has the full measure when it comes to glamour."

"And she can be very funny," Delia timidly offered. There was a lot to be said for being funny.

"Never more than when she isn't aware of it," Blaine delicately mocked.

"She's a *hex!*" Hilary tilted her small freckled nose into the air. "She's not an Angel, either. Far from it." Hilary was well into her stride, wanting to claw and slash whenever Genni's name was mentioned. "Genni is the angelic-looking one. So beautiful and bright and innocent. *Innocent?* Why she's as sexy as they come. I bet she's no virgin, either. Not with all those boyfriends hanging 'round her."

Blaine, at the head of the gleaming mahogany table, suddenly squared his wide shoulders, fixing Hilary with a diamond-hard glance. "It's not often I've sent you from the table, Hilary. After all, you're supposed to be an adult. But you can excuse yourself right now."

At the forcefulness of his tone an expression of real fright touched Hilary's dark eyes. She rose so awkwardly she sent her long-stemmed wineglass, which only contained mineral water, over. "That's right. Go on," she flounced, furious tears springing into her eyes. "You should have been Genni's Black Knight. So you can defend her to the death."

As Delia was officially mistress of Jubilee Downs, the planning and organization of the Polo Weekend and the culminating Gala Ball should have fallen to her, but such were her lack of organisational skills and interest in a game that excited great Outback passions; a game at which her late husband and her stepson excelled, since her return to her family home, Lally had taken all responsibility out of Delia's grateful hands. The result was whenever it was Jubilee's turn to hold meets and ultimately if their team won the Gala Ball, everything went exceedingly well. Nevertheless Lally, who wasn't getting any younger, and the number of people, teams and spectators who attended, always getting larger, she was very appreciative of Genni's offer to help.

Genni was very methodical, like herself. She undertook whatever she had to do with great care and energy. Lally never had to tell her the same thing twice. She had grown up with it, soaking up the whole exciting atmosphere like a sponge. It made up somehow for the disappointment Lally felt at Delia's and her young niece's lack of excitement in the event, although Hilary since she had grown up looked forward to the ball.

Delia, on the other hand, was shy by nature. She didn't feel comfortable with crowds of people. She found it difficult to make small talk with people she didn't know. She was the complete opposite of Blaine's beautiful mother, Crystelle. The very reason my poor brother married her, Lally thought. Crystelle, beautiful, brilliant, had fled him, unable to cope with the isolation of station life. Delia, quiet and retiring, was a woman who could be counted on to stay put. Lally had grown genuinely fond of Delia but she deplored Delia's lack of parental control over her mercurial daughter.

Hilary's tantrums were becoming increasingly exhausting although she had been on her best behaviour since Blaine had so clearly shown his displeasure. Hilary had gone down to the station airstrip to welcome Angel's party when they flew in. She had greeted Angel and Genni with a rare peck on the cheek, been respectful to Toby Slocombe, a big, slightly over-weight man with a very nice smile and shrewd intelligent eyes, and somewhat flirtatious with Genni's beau, Colin Garrett of the soft floppy hair and crinkling hazel eyes. Genni had asked and been given permission to bring him. Lally only hoped the pleasantness would last.

"It must have taken a lot of work to keep the grass so green and velvety in the heat," Genni's musical voice broke into Lally's thoughts. They were working in the utility room of the kitchen, finishing off the flower arrangements.

Lally nodded with satisfaction. "I got the boys to follow Blaine's advice." When Blaine had time, he was around to supervise. "I worry about Blaine. He works too hard." Lally stood back to admire a huge Chinese vase she had filled with soaring branches of white bauhinia. The orchid-like flowers would fall soon enough but for a day or two the arrangement would look magical. "The going can't be too tough, as we know," she continued. "Can't jar the ponies legs. On the other hand if the turf is too soft it will slow them down. Where's your boyfriend, by the way?"

"He's deserted me for Blaine." Genni smiled. "Blaine has that effect on people. The last time I saw them Blaine was showing Colin and Toby around the field, explaining things to them, I expect. Neither of them knows the game. Afterwards he was going to take them down to the stables to see the ponies. You've done a wonderful job, Lally." Genni slipped her arm around the older woman, momentarily leaning her ash-blond head affectionately against Lally's. "I've missed you."

"I've missed you, too, girl." Lally not terribly used to physical demonstrations of affection spoke a little stiffly, but her regal face wore a poignant expression, a combination of pleasure and sadness, perhaps at her own childless state. "Do you like all the flags I've put up around the grounds?" she asked, clearing her throat slightly.

"They look great." Genni, understanding Lally very well, went back to her own work. "So does the new way you've placed all the tables and chairs under the trees. It looks like an al fresco restaurant. The Great Hall looks marvellous, too. You must have been very very busy, especially with Delia and Hilary away."

"I'm glad of something to do," Lally confided. "I changed my mind a couple of times about the decoration of the hall. Sure you like it?"

"Of course I do." Genni smiled encouragement. "You have great taste, Lally. It's all so wonderfully exciting, isn't it? Colin's over the moon. He's never been outback before. He loves everything he sees."

"Is it serious with Colin?" Lally asked, inwardly shying away from a "yes" answer.

"We're fairly close. I'm just enjoying myself, Lally," Genni answered blithely. "Colin is very easy to be with. He's a lot of fun and he knows how to get around Angel."

"What man doesn't?" Lally snorted, tucking a stray silver-grey lock back into the easy French pleat she had worn for years now.

"Don't be naughty," Genni scolded her, waving a forefinger.

"And Mr. Slocombe?" Lally flipped Genni a sparkling glance.

"Aaah! Now that *could* be serious." Genni dropped her head owlishly. "At least Angel is hoping so."

"She's likely to have as many husbands as Elizabeth Taylor," Lally, husbandless, offered dryly, but not without a certain small envy.

"Oh, don't say that!" Genni implored. "I'm having trouble keeping up as it is. Actually Angel introduced Colin to me. I think you could safely say she's given him the thumbs up. His father is George Garrett. You know, the Freight King?" Genni stopped to get Lally's attention.

Lally looked back dry as ash. "I guessed as much. Don't let your mother push you into anything you don't want, darling girl. She's good at that. A born manipulator."

"She only wants the best for me, Lally." Genni shook her head, ever loyal. "At least in her own way. She hasn't really grasped we're completely different. Neither for that matter has Blaine."

Lally stopped what she was doing, anxious to get her message across. "Now take it easy with Blaine this weekend, hear? He has enough to put up with with young Hilary."

"Lally, dearest, I'm going to do my level best. As for Hilary, she'll settle down given enough time. Life here is too remote for her. She's not a bush person."

"She really doesn't have anything of her father in her." Lally clicked her tongue. "Just between the two of us," Lally leaned closer, "Delia lets her get away with murder."

"An only child?" Genni excused, cautiously.

"What are you two whispering about?" a familiar male voice demanded from the doorway. A dark-timbered voice that caused a rush of goose bumps down Genni's arms.

She swung her blond head, caught at the nape with a deep blue ribbon. She had a sudden irresistible urge to reach out and hug him like she used to, instead she said casually, "Hi!"

"Hi yourself?" His beautiful smile flashed over her as he moved into the room with his characteristic easy grace. A plain white T-shirt stretched over his wide taut chest, beautiful muscular forearms, tight-fitting blue jeans, lean, long flanks. Sexy as hell. "Missed you at breakfast."

"I went for a ride." She didn't say she'd hoped to catch up with him. "Didn't anyone tell you?"

"Actually Lollypop did the moment I walked into the stables." Lollypop was the part aboriginal stable hand so called because of his habit of always juggling a lollypop in his mouth. "He also told me you took The Boxer?"

"That's okay, isn't it?" She spoke sweetly, mindful of Lally's request.

"I don't know." Blaine rubbed his cleft chin, his good-health skin gleaming in the golden light from the open windows. "He's proving a bit tricky. I think I'll have to have him gelded. I know you're a good rider, having taught you *very well*—" he exaggerated "—myself, but I'd prefer it if you stuck with Aurora for this visit. Okay?"

She moved nearer to him to sketch a little series of Arabian gestures. "Your wish is my command," she murmured submissively.

"Really?"

For a moment it seemed to Genni he was gazing right *into* her, so unaccountably she flushed. "Absolutely."

"I intend to remind you of that one of these days, violet eyes." Languidly he leaned over and tugged one of her curls.

"I have complete confidence you will. So where did you leave Colin and Toby?"

"Ah, Colin and Toby! The boyfriends!" His silver glance was mocking. "I'm sure I remember them."

"I assure you they're very impressed with you. And your style of living."

"You wouldn't lie to me, would you, Genni?" Another half smile, his teeth superbly white. "Anyway, Toby couldn't have gone more than a minute before Angel came looking for him. I let Colin have one of the Jeeps. He wants to take a look around but he's promised not go out too far. I don't want to have to go looking for him."

She turned her slender body to stare directly at him. "Are you sure?"

"What are you accusing me of?" he challenged. "Of course I'm sure. I make it my business to look after your boyfriends."

"Oh-ho and what about Josh Hamilton?" This time her tone was tart.

"Don't remember the name." His laugh was low but far from gentle. "These arrangements are really beautiful." He walked about, looking at what they'd done. "I especially like this." He dipped his dark head to smell the ravishing fragrance of a mix of summer flowers, his mouth almost touching a rose petal. For some reason Genni's heart contracted. Blaine could be so damned…erotic at times. Or so it struck her.

"Genni's work," Lally told him with pride. "She's an artistic genius."

"You and me both!" Genni, putting an arm around Lally's trim waist, embraced her. "You know the lovely life-size marble lady in the entrance hall, I thought I'd place this arrangement in her hand?" She looked to Blaine for his opinion, indicating a charming small arrangement of yellow roses, butter-yellow ranunculus, little sprigs of wattle with touches of green.

"Why not? A lady should constantly receive flowers from an admirer. Let me do it." He glanced at Lally and smiled. "I guess I'll be horrified at the bill?"

"Comfort yourself, my dear, a surprising amount came from the home gardens. I've had Fred and his helpers working hard. The rest, the more delicate blooms, all the blues and mauves and lilacs were flown in. We've had them in the cold room."

"So where's Hilary?" He cocked a brow. "I asked her to give you a hand."

"That's okay. Genni and I managed."

"Brilliantly by the look of it." Blaine glanced in Genni's direction. "I'm on my way over to the Great Hall. Do you want to come?"

"Sure. Lally can't handle positioning all these vases, though."

"We're not going to ask her. I'll do it before we go."

"Listen you two," Lally clucked fondly, so much wanting them to spend time together, "I've got Ruby and the girls to help me." She referred to Jubilee's long-time housekeeper and her small well-trained domestic staff. "So leave. Go enjoy yourselves and remember what I told you, Genni."

"Yes, Lally dearest!" Genni gave her a cheeky wave from the door.

So like her mother. So unlike her mother. Stephen was there too, Lally thought.

* * *

Moments later they were out in the hot sunshine, walking away from the magnificent double-storied homestead with its balconies and pillared verandas and cast-iron lace balustrade, towards what the family called the Great Hall, a multi-purpose building used for meetings, cattle conventions, family weddings, balls and parties, even a glamorous show ring to show off the highly sought-after polo ponies bred by the station and offered at packed sales.

"So what did Lally tell you?" Blaine questioned, glancing down at Genni's lovely tranquil profile.

"A secret!" She put a finger to her lips, almost dancing to keep up with his long stride.

"Some secret. I bet she told you to be sweet to me."

"I mean to be." She gave him a provocative little smirk.

"And no one sweeter when you choose."

"That goes for you, too." She smiled at him in a way even she didn't realize. "I love you when you're not up on your high horse. So what do you think of Colin? Tell me, I'm dying to know."

He gave a mock yawn. "Who?"

"Pleeze!" She angled a mocking glance.

He laughed shortly. "Likeable. Nice manners. Certainly an improvement on some of the others."

"In case you're interested, it's not serious." So why had she said that when she and Colin had been an item for months now? She didn't want to know.

"I wasn't thinking he was your lover?" Blaine's downbent glance was so searing it burned.

"Listen. I don't think you'd approve of anyone I wanted to marry?" she challenged, realising in some confusion she couldn't bear to think of Sally Fenwick as Blaine's future bride, either.

"I guess I've played the role of Big Brother for too long," Blaine murmured, his voice a shade metallic.

"Anyway, Colin is just a friend. For now." Her heart was pumping like she was telling lies.

"I'll take your word for it."

She flickered a glance at him. He was so absolutely beautiful to her, like some godlike creature. "Oh, let's be friends!" She grasped his arm in an excess of brittle joy, hugging it the way she used to. "I've so been looking forward to this weekend."

"Me, too," he murmured, but his expression was unreadable.

They were almost at the hall when the sound of an approaching aircraft resonated in the air. "Another plane coming in." Genni turned her head skywards as the light aircraft began to circle the homestead on its way to the station airstrip. Light aircraft carrying guests had been landing all morning, dotting the fields to either side. "Do I know them?"

Blaine shaded his eyes. "Sure you do. That's the Camerons. I expect they're all travelling together."

"Great. It's been a long time. Oh, goodness!" Genni broke off lowering her head protectively as a strong breeze blew down the canyon of the outbuildings, catching her ribbon, tugging it from her hair as debris blew into her eye.

She moaned.

"Oh, hell!" Instantly Blaine turned her the other way, sheltering her with his body, while the air settled down.

"There's something in my eye."

"Here, let me. No, don't rub it in." He drew her beneath a broad awning, pulling a handkerchief out of his jeans' pocket. "This is perfectly clean. Stand still, cherub. Lift your head. Look at me."

"I can't." She blinked, dreading the notion she might have a red eye for the party.

"Be brave." There was a smile in his voice.

"Oh, go on then." Genni held up her face, widening her

eyes, the tip of her pink tongue pressed against her bowed upper lip to assist her concentration.

Deftly Blaine twisted his white handkerchief into a little peak, gently foraging for the dark speck. "I've got it!" he announced with considerable satisfaction, looking down at her when inexplicably his whole body turned as taut as piano wire. She could feel the abrupt change through his hand.

What was up?

Genni held her position for a moment while she blinked several times. "That's better." She opened her eyes to smile up at him only to encounter a gaze so full of strange glittering lights she was dazzled, unnerved. "Blaine?" Her voice wobbled, as tremulous as a child's.

There was a sharp, very difficult pause. A moment of revelation so potent it was almost a terror. Every pulse in her body quickened. She couldn't look away yet they stood in this ongoing radiant white silence, until Blaine reached out and put his hands on her slender hips and drew her towards him. On this day of days there were people all over the station yet the whole world emptied to just the two of them. Hushed.

"You want me to tell you something?" she whispered, trembling and shaking. "You can be very frightening at times."

"Like now?"

She almost sank to her knees in shock. The Blaine she knew had assumed another shape, so powerful, so intoxicating it was like being taken over. Possessed. A pulse beat wildly in her throat. Her small breasts rose steeply beneath her silk shirt. Sexual sensations were whispering and humming all over her skin like little currents of electricity, drawing a small moan to her lips. "What are you doing?" Her violet eyes darkened, a flush like crushed rose petals stained her cheeks.

Doing? God, he was as shaken as she was, but hiding it much better. He knew he should stop. She wasn't ready for this but his own will was dissolving under a weight of tenderness and a tremendous rush of desire that clouded his judgment. This was Genni. She was forbidden to him. Which was total rubbish. Then again, he wasn't feeling rational. Her breath smelled of apples, sweet and fresh. The tip of her tongue was a leaf around which his own ached to twine.

She was so beautiful. So desperately beautiful, the substance of dreams, with her masses of white-gold hair cascading around her shoulders and down her back, those violet eyes imploring him not to risk altering everything in a minute. Their whole relationship.

He could see her little convulsive swallows but that didn't stop him arching her imperceptibly closer. How pliant was her slender body. How delicately executed. He wanted to bring up a hand, slip a pearly button on the pale silk of her beautiful shirt. He wanted to expose a small exquisite breast, bring his mouth to the tightly budded nipple, so clearly betraying; peaked against the gossamer-light material. She was looking back at him tortured, bewitched, her self-possession all gone. He wanted to kiss her open-mouthed. All the kisses they had exchanged over the years. Scattered pecks. Sometimes tight little extravagant smacks when she arrived. "Home sweet home!"

This kiss would be different. Unlike any kiss she had ever received before in her life. He would fold his mouth over hers, finding it as lush and pulsing as ever a man dreamed of, pressing down harder…deeper and deeper, drinking her in as if from a glistening life-giving spring.

God help him, he wanted her so badly in a moment he would haul her to him. Pick her up. Carry her away, Precious Genni. Her power over him was spellbinding.

Unsuspecting of the scene that was unravelling, Hilary and Sally Fenwick in tow rounded a corner, they, too, on their way to the Great Hall. Their jaws fell open to see Genni standing perfectly still under Blaine's hands, yet poised like a creature too mesmerized to take flight. Blaine's gleaming black head was bent over her in an attitude so intense, so sexual it was like the two of them were enveloped in clouds of smoke.

"Oh, great heavens!" poor Sally cried, feeling seared to the bone, but unable to look away. "Let's go back," she begged, clutching at Hilary's hand.

"Don't be silly." Hilary gave a small dangerous smile. "Don't you know Genni does this all the time?"

"Does what?" Sally's halting voice shook. She had always liked Genni. They got on extremely well.

"Genni loves playing these little flirting games," Hilary explained, making no attempt to hide her disgust. "She's like her mother. It doesn't mean anything. She's as good as engaged to the guy she brought with her."

"Is she?" Sally who'd adored Blaine Courtland for most of her life and really felt she had a chance with him, forced some air into her depleted lungs. "If you ask me it's Genni who should be protected."

"From whom?" Hilary snapped, in her own private hell.

"Why…Blaine. He looks like he's about to drag her off like a caveman. He never looks like that with me."

"You don't understand Blaine," Hilary responded grimly. "He has to be lord and master. What you're seeing doesn't mean *a thing*. You're the girl Blaine has in his sights. Genni is family."

It was far from Sally's conclusion. Not now. What she had understood to be their relationship—cousins—had been brutally swept aside. They looked like lovers. Sally couldn't really comprehend it. She felt shell-shocked.

The two teams cantered out onto the field to thunderous high-spirited cheers that circled and rose into the clear desert air to startle the birds. Four men to a team, wearing the traditional

helmet, jersey, snowy-white breeches, high glossy-black
boots. The championship had already been won by Blaine's
team, the impressive silver cup displayed on the library table
in the homestead's entrance hall. This was an exhibition
match to add to the excitement and unashamed glamour of
the weekend.

For the first chukka, Blaine was riding a magnificent
chestnut gelding whose hide gleamed like satin in the brilliant sunshine. His team wore a distinctive red-and-black
jersey piped with white; the opposition, emerald-green and
navy.

Genni couldn't look away from Blaine though she had
seen him playing countless times. He looked magnificent in
the saddle, a veritable paragon of masculine dash and daring.
Quick thinking, physically and mentally tough with all the
shots, this had earned him his usual position as Number Two.
His job as the most influential attacking player, to work
closely with his Number One, the front player, keeping the
ball moving up the field which today thanks to a lot of hard
work looked velvety green. They were playing a full match
divided into six seven-minute chukkas. Each player needed a
string of ponies, at least three, as no pony due to the rigorous
demands of the game was ever used for more than two con-
secutive chukkas. It was this that made the game so expensive to play.

"Gosh, these guys are really something!" Colin raised his
brows and whistled, turning to smile at Genni, who was re-
clining comfortable in a deck chair. They had found a deliciously cool spot beneath the trees, their gourmet hamper to
one side, a bottle of champers on ice. "Why didn't you tell
me your cousin was such a glamorous character?" he chortled,
quite without envy. One of the nicest things about him. "You
don't see guys like that all that often. Hell, he looks like a film
star playing a polo player in a movie. And would you listen
to all those females shrieking his name."

"He doesn't hear them, believe me," Genni offered very dryly, knowing it to be true.

"It'd go right to my head," Colin freely admitted, taking a gulp of eucalypt fragrant air. "Say, this is the life! A gorgeous girl, champers, hampers and a jolly good game of polo." He tried his best pukka accent. "Never thought I'd enjoy myself so much. It must be a powerful thing to rule over your own kingdom. Which as far as I can see is pretty much what your cousin does."

Genni's eyes were shaded by her designer sunglasses. "He takes the job very seriously, Colin. Jubilee, like the other famous stations, is our pioneering history."

"Yes, indeed! I had to see it to believe it!" Colin was thoroughly enjoying himself. "And that homestead! They sure know how to live. He's a wonderful rider. I expect he'd have to be born in the saddle."

"True but they don't all ride so elegantly. You'll see just how good Blaine is when they start to play. Blaine and his horse move as one. The accord between man and pony is total. It doesn't happen overnight. Blaine puts a lot of his time into training his ponies. It takes a lot of work."

"They don't look like ponies to me." Colin's eyes surveyed the teams' mounts. "They look more like they belong at the races."

"Blaine's mount is a thoroughbred. So are most of the others. A couple of three-quarter thoroughbreds.

"Polo mounts are always referred to as ponies," Genni explained. "Pony is just a term. Blaine reads the game better than most. He's a great one for tactics." On and off the field, she thought with a pang of the heart. "That's what won them the cup. Both teams were excellent but Blaine brought the better tactics to bear."

"What's the big sigh for?" Colin turned to her in surprise. "It sounded like it came from deep inside you."

"Oh, sometimes Blaine can be overwhelming," Genni found herself confessing.

Colin considered briefly. "I can see that. He's been very nice to me, though."

"He likes you."

"Great!" Colin's attractive grin lit up his face. "I'm damned sure you and I won't be going places unless we have your cousin onside." Colin reached out and took Genni's hand, carrying it to his lips. "You look good enough to eat. A delicious strawberry-and-vanilla gelato."

Genni was wearing linen pants with a matching sleeveless shirt in a vivid shade of pink, her head and her eyes protected by a large floppy hat in finest cream straw, the brim decorated with pink full-blown roses.

"Mmm!" He began to lick the back of her hand. "What are you wearing tonight? Something seriously sexy I hope?"

"Collette Dinnigan. Your only clue."

"That's enough!" Colin smiled broadly, then lay back. "I just love a woman to look like a woman. Appealing but revealing. You do things to me, Genni, no one has ever done before. I love being with you. I'm beginning to think I need to be with you all the time."

Exhibition game or not the match was played at a furious pace, individual daring bringing the heart into the throat. At halftime, with the goals equal, Genni stayed well back, not going up to Blaine to have a word as she had done for years but watching proceedings from her leafy shelter beneath the trees.

Blaine was busy changing his jersey, unconsciously displaying his great physical shape still not registering the oohs and aahs and burst of girlish giggles around the field.

Colin had gone off to speak to one of the spectators he recognised from back in his college days, so she was able to sit quietly trying to understand what had happened only a few short hours before. Whatever it was it amounted to a crisis point. The world around her had changed. Even Colin. She thought she was in love with him. Or love as she had understood it. Now she was horribly confused.

Ignorance is bliss.

Across the field she saw Sally Fenwick, even at a distance flushed with pleasure, tall and athletic in very trendy dress-up denim go up to Blaine, put her arms around him and kiss his cheek. Perhaps a lot more shyly than Sally usually did. But then Sally and Hilary had witnessed that odd scene outside the Great Hall where hers and Blaine's emotions had inexplicably got out of hand. Blaine had been sufficiently in control of himself to recover in a moment, but she had continued to stand there in a daze, as Sally and Hilary continued down the walkway to join them.

Hilary's dark eyes had flashed the usual getting-to-be-boring message, "I hate you!" Sally, who was really very nice, had tried her familiar friendly smile but underneath Genni knew she was stricken. As well she might be. Sally had hung in there far longer than any of the others. Sally knew what she wanted out of life. That want was Blaine Courtland.

Play was due to start again. Colin returned, coming up behind her, laying his hands possessively on her shoulders. "Miss me, darling?"

"No, not at all!" She gave him a backward smile. "You were only gone ten minutes."

"If you loved me that's long enough, you know." Colin, his clean shiny hair flopping onto his forehead, bent over her, dropping a lingering kiss on her mouth.

All of which was noticed on and around the field.

CHAPTER FOUR

The Polo Ball

CLOUDLESS heavens. A billion glittering desert stars. The Milky Way a jewel-encrusted ribbon. Over the homestead roof. The Southern Cross, the Guiding One, in all its unique magic.

Inside the house there was still a huge crowd although the ball was already under way, the sound of the band's music carrying strongly on the night air.

Blaine made his way through the whirling crowd, submitting to one fervent embrace after the other. Lots of cooing. Arms flung wide in greeting.

"Blaine, daaarling, you've been ignoring me!"

"Blaine, promise you're going to dance with me!"

"Daaarling Blaine, you look simply divine in evening clothes!"

Wafts of expensive perfume, pretty mouths, pretty teeth, colourful rustling dresses. What man in his right mind would object to being pounded on by a bevy of very attractive young women who left him in no doubt of their feelings. All of them his for the asking. It filled him with no sense of triumph. Only a kind of bittersweet longing for that one woman he knew could fill his heart.

With practised sardonic charm Blaine made his way

through the main reception rooms, gratified the homestead was looking its very best, all the while wondering where Genni was. Genni unlike her mother had never been one for staging an entrance. She should be down by now. He wanted to direct everyone over to the Great Hall.

He had barely reached the entrance hall when he heard a male voice call out, There's Genni!" There was so much delight in the tone, he was searingly conscious he, too, was experiencing an enormous inner quickening.

Genni.

So then he looked up at her.

She was standing at the first landing of the grand curving staircase, her lovely face brilliant in animation, smiling and waving, radiating so perfectly the sheer pleasure and excitement of the evening.

How was it, he wondered, when he had barely noticed what the other women wore he took in every last detail of Genni's appearance? She had her beautiful hair long and loose, the way he liked best, the front caught up in some arrangement adorned with a jewelled clip. Her dress was a beautiful shade of blue, echoing her eyes, the filmy fabric sewn with swirls of the same colour sequins. Here and there full-blown deep pink silk roses were embroidered. He realized the cut was pretty much as revealing as a slip, but much more romantic, a barely there kind of dress with a crossover skirt that showed off one long slender leg and her exquisite evening sandals. His breath caught hard and fast. He felt a powerful tide of pride in her. And possession. This was his Genni. He had always had such joy in her. He wanted to claim her. Shut her away from the sight of any other man. God, it almost amused him he was in such a vulnerable state of mind.

Genni, looking down at the sea of faces, all bright and smiling, suddenly realized she was intent on singling out a particular glinting gaze. Suddenly she saw him. He was standing near the tall double doors that led to the drawing room, a strangely handsome, commanding kind of man.

And there it was again, a recurrence of the afternoon. A look of naked sensuality barely veiled in his upturned silver glance.

Oh, God, she hadn't misread it. Just as she hadn't misread it hours before. Once again she was left reeling: alarmed and feverishly excited by the impact of a single glance. There was such a thrilling quality about Blaine. A physical exhilaration that on these occasions made her legs go weak and her throat go dry. She knew she was looking back questioningly at him, feeling the heat in her cheeks. Whatever lifetime of affection that had lain between them was being invaded by a powerful sense of something else. What? Genni, heart hammering, felt she had entered another country.

And then he smiled. His rare slow, magical smile that lit his dark face to radiance.

She smiled back. Nope, he only meant he was proud of her. Even as her heartbeats began to settle, and the panic that had washed her started to subside, she felt a profound pang of disappointment. Disappointment at what? At what precise moment had her view of her childhood hero changed? He was still her hero, whether they truly got on or not, but she couldn't begin to wrestle with all these other treacherous emotions that were crowding her, backing her against a brick wall. What had never been could not be. He was toying with her. He had a dark streak.

Genni walked down the thickly carpeted Persian runner marshalling her defences against that all-powerful figure in her life. Her arrogant cousin Blaine. She was still physically dizzy but she held her head high. Not for the first time it occurred to her Blaine was a very dangerous man. And judging from the expressions on the faces of the young women surrounding him her own fascination was echoed over and over. In a word, Blaine was dynamite.

When she reached the lowest step he had made his way through the crowd, who despersed like magic at his approach, to put out a lazy hand. "Now the ball can begin."

His silver eyes still sparkled with something Genni hadn't the courage to name. "You look wonderful," she said, deliberately keeping her voice sweet and cousinly, relieved beyond words it sounded just that.

"You were the prettiest little girl I've ever seen," he drawled. "You still are." It was a near physical kiss. His mouth on hers.

God! A million stars burst inside her. He was wicked! "Part of me loves you." she whispered very softly, leaning her white-gold head in towards him. "The best part. So be agreeable tonight."

"And you behave yourself, as well," he clipped off, lifting her hand to kiss it, ignoring if he even noticed the tremble in her white fingers. He drew her towards the door, calling to everyone to follow them to the Great Hall.

Out on the veranda, Colin came rushing up the short flight of steps, exclaiming as he came, "Genni, baby, I thought you'd never get dressed. I've been waiting for you for ages. You look gorgeous!" Colin closed in on them but Blaine didn't relinquish Genni's arm, the set of his wide shoulders beneath the fine cloth of his dinner jacket and a certain routine imperious expression indicating Colin wasn't going to claim his "girlfriend" for a while. Colin in high good spirits made do by walking alongside, thanking Blaine over and over for being "so darn nice" as to invite him. He was having a whale of a time.

By ten o'clock the ball was in full swing. From the network of beams in the Great Hall with its huge cathedral-like space, hung a spectacular lineup of polo flags of all countries, their bold bright colours lighting up the area. Appended from the lowest beams were great double-sided framed action shots of that year's championships match taken by an Outback photographer who had become internationally famous. One could see why. The photographs were a triumph; so glamorous and romantic. Genni's eye gravitated to them time and time again. She loved the shots featuring Blaine, particularly one that caught him at the precise moment, arm held aloft, when he was preparing to square cut a ball. His chestnut pony's two front legs were well clear of the ground, Blaine's two team-mates had fallen back to give him room for the full free swing that was to score the deciding goal.

"A real winner, isn't it?" Lally, regal in navy lace, a beautiful turquoise and pearl choker 'round her throat turned to Genni, a flush of pleasure on her face at the success of the evening.

"No doubt about it." Warmly Genni slipped an arm through Lally's. "It really takes hold of the imagination. Everyone's having a wonderful time. Isn't that great!"

"I'm so pleased." Lally's fine eyes were twinkling. "Even our little Hilary has been won around, but I think her dress is wrong. I'm not sure why. It's beautiful enough."

"Maybe just a little too sophisticated," Genni said thoughtfully. "But she looks lovely and she's in such a good mood."

"Which she should be all the time of course." Lally's voice sharpened a fraction. "Given how much is done for her."

"There goes Angel!" Genni interrupted, giving her mother a little wave as she and Toby Slocombe boogied past. No old-fashioned fox trots for Angel. She was absolutely up to the minute. She had caused a sensation when she had first appeared in her Chanel couture strapless number with tiers and tiers of ruffles for a skirt, a huge scarlet silk camellia fixed to a white shoulder, a billion-dollar smile on her face.

"Sometimes I think she deserves a twenty-one gun salute," Blaine had quipped at the time.

Now Genni and Lally looked with pleasure around the dance floor. As usual the women had gone to town, grateful for the opportunity to dress up and look beautiful for their men. Every colour of the rainbow was on the floor, pinks, blues, purples, lots of floral patterns and appliqués. Sequins and paillettes caught every turn of the huge revolving disco light, setting the metallic dresses from silver to bronze and glitzy gold to pure dazzle.

Across the room Sally Fenwick, head thrown back, naked back arched, was riding a wave of pleasure locked in Blaine's arms. He must have been saying something amusing because Sally was laughing joyously, the sound coming clearly over the buzz of conversation and the loudness of the band. Whatever he had told her about that odd scene she and Hilary had stumbled on, Sally had been prepared to believe it. Or maybe Hilary had convinced her it had been her fault. Blaine looked relaxed. Probably telling Sally how wonderful she looked, which she did, though her strapless electric blue satin dress was falling perilously low and Sally had an eye-catching full bosom. Not that any man present would take exception to that, Genni thought.

Both women turned as Colin returned, holding the cold drink Genni had requested. Even with all the doors and windows opened, and many fans circling, the crush of people had raised the temperature in the hall.

"Here you are, beautiful." Colin smiled at Genni with great pride and pleasure, thinking how exquisitely beautiful she looked. No wonder his father had congratulated him on winning Genni's affections. He wondered how she would react if he popped the question. Feeling all warm and reckless, Colin still remembered to turn to Lally. "Could I get anything for you, Miss Lally?" he asked courteously, slightly in awe of Miss Eulalia Courtland though she had been very gracious.

"No thank you, my dear." She shook her elegantly coiffured head. "I must see about supper." With a nod and a smile Lally moved off, looking around for a particular friend with whom she wanted to have a word. The ball was in full swing. She thought the first wave for supper should be timed for another half hour. She only hoped the gossip columnist who usually came along to these affairs wouldn't use the word "sumptuous" in connection with the supper, though it undoubtedly was.

"Let's take a whirl, princess," Colin put his arm around Genni's waist, steering her towards the dance floor. "I need to hold you in my arms."

Genni laughed as she looked up at him. "Do you know you've developed an Outback drawl?"

"Specially for you, darlin'." Colin gathered her in close, revelling in her femininity and the magnificent chaos of white-gold curls that fell over his arm. "This little trip has been marvellous for me. It's settled a lot of things in my mind."

"Like what," Genni said, almost conversationally.

"Like what would marriage be like to a beautiful warm-hearted girl like you?" Colin could feel himself excited as he said it. He even felt a smidgeon of the old familiar panic.

Genni wasn't certain if he was serious or not. "You're not letting this go to your head, are you, Colin? I thought you didn't see yourself as a husband?" Most people perceived Colin Garrett as a playboy.

"Maybe not in the past. But now... I can't give you up." Colin's gaze grew soft and serious. At that moment he believed himself deeply in love. He couldn't remember feeling quite like that before. He had to do something. On a rush of emotion, he bent his head and kissed Genni very lingeringly on the mouth, feeling her lips open like velvety petals. She was perfect to kiss. *Perfect!* It wouldn't be too long before he could get her into bed with him. She hadn't much liked the idea up to date.

"Did you see that?" A distance away, Hilary, standing momentarily with her stepbrother, felt she had been handed a golden opportunity. "Genni has finally fallen in love," she gulped. "I never thought it was going to happen. She loves to play the field."

"Really?" Blaine sounded distant. He followed her gaze, as did most people. "That's a bit of a refrain of yours isn't it, Hilary?" He looked across the swirling sea of celebrating couples to where Colin and Genni were clasped in each other's arms. They appeared to be rocking gently on the spot, apparently oblivious to everyone around them. "It's a fact of life beautiful young women get pursued."

"Oh quite!" Hilary responded in high glee. "Only this time it looks like Colin is going to catch her. Did you ever see two people so totally engaged in each other? Genni told me she was *very* interested." She stared up at Blaine to gauge his reaction, finding his handsome face set in lines of disbelief.

"When did she tell you that? I don't think you've spent more than five minutes together," he scoffed.

"How would you know?" She kept her tone sweet and reasonable. "You weren't around most of the time. You were playing polo. She told me this afternoon after the match."

"They're just friends." Blaine sounded very definite. Too definite for Hilary, who was determined to make mischief.

She grasped her stepbrother's jacketed arm, standing on tiptoes to whisper confidentially, "I can tell you she's working hard to convince you of that. I don't know *why* exactly. She actually warned me to keep quiet. You have to admit she doesn't like you to know what she's up to. You object such a lot. She'll tell you, all right, when it's too late for you to do anything about it. Anyway I like him. And he wants Genni so much. Anyone can see that."

"At least two hundred and fifty people, I'd say." Typically Blaine sounded sardonic.

In the next moment a partner came to claim Hilary and she moved triumphantly out onto the floor. Every chance she got to come between Blaine and Genni she was going to take. She'd lived too many years in the shadow of Genni's glory.

He waited until Colin had left Genni's side for a brief moment before he made his move.

"Is it my imagination or have you been avoiding me?" He closed each of his fingers around her silky bare arm.

"I think I probably have." Feeling as she did she wasn't about to lie.

"Why?" He moved her out onto the dance floor, knowing it was a mistake.

"You damned well know why. You can't blame me." His arms around her made her feel physically weak. So weak it was like some powerful drug had hit her bloodstream. Although she appeared as cool as a lily, inwardly she was swept by a wave of high emotion. She felt like she was standing on a ledge. Unprotected. What game was Blaine playing? She would die of humiliation if he was only trying to prove his control over her. Didn't he know he tore the heart from her?

He held her in silence *for* a few moments, bodies close, Genni feeling so shivery she burst out spontaneously, "I don't know if I can bear this." A dead give-away, but she couldn't control it.

His long arm tightened. "Bear what? Don't even think of trying to make a fool of me, Violetta."

His old nickname for her sparked many complex feelings. "That wouldn't do would it?"

"Not when everybody's having such a good time. Why are you afraid to talk to me?"

He was such a wonderful mover. A natural. He made Colin seem flat-footed. "I'm upset, that's why," she admitted, staring over his shoulder.

"Really, I would have said just the reverse. That little love scene with Garrett was worth watching."

"Maybe he's just the sort of man I need," she answered desperately.

"I can't think how you arrived at that conclusion." His voice was coolly level. "Although I have to concede he can be charming in a very boyish sort of way."

He might have patted her on the head. The arrogance! "You're not going to give up, are you?"

"Give up?" His tone was silky. "Give *you* up?"

"Yes, yes, yes. It's outrageous how you interfere in my life."

"Interference, is that what it's called? Genni, you amaze me."

"Blaine, please." She raised her violet eyes to him. "I'm finding this very painful. Can we stop dancing?"

"Not for a moment. I want to hear something. Did you or did you not tell Hilary you were *very interested* in Colin?"

Her deep sigh expressed despair. "I shall scream if you don't let me go," she said emotionally, so powerfully conscious of him and his body it was simply excruciating.

"No you won't, Genni," he said quietly, but his eyes crackled with light.

"I'm tempted." She threw her head back to stare at him.

"Of course you're tempted. You feel threatened. But you obviously don't want to talk about it."

Wasn't *that* the truth? She was terrified of opening up a Pandora's box. "May I point out Sally is sulking over there."

He sounded amused. "Sally never sulks."

"Oh, for God's sake, I know." She conceded that with a little shake of the head. "But she's obviously missing you." Sally was in fact waving her arms rather wildly, perhaps under the influence of too much champagne. Genni waved back, trying to put a bright reassuring smile on her face. "Is that your orchid she has pinned to her dress?"

"It is." Blaine eased her away from a jitter-bugging couple. "Sally greatly fancies orchids."

"Well you'd know." Her beauty was heightened by a flow of colour to her cheeks. "You go back a long way."

He stared at her. "How fascinating. You sound jealous."

Resolutely she looked away. "Don't be ridiculous. I like Sally. You'd better go and dance with her."

"I'm having a good time as it is dancing with my favour-ite cousin."

"Not the *whole* damn time."

"*Always,*" he mocked. "In all your moods. How absolutely beautiful you look tonight. Did I tell you?"

Her whole body vibrated. "I certainly don't remember."

"Well I'm telling you now. I so love that dress."

Something in his voice was moving her to tears. "We're too close, aren't we, Blaine," she astounded herself by saying. "Too dangerously close. I'm finally beginning to understand your hold over me." She looked up at him, finding his glance brilliant, searching, mocking? She loved him. Oh, yes! Half hated him, as well. It was difficult to construct her true picture of Blaine. He had played so many roles.

The music stopped, the band struck up again, this time a brighter upbeat tempo.

"I should get back to Colin." She took the opportunity to spring away.

"Why not?" He stood back, a suggestion of sizzling anger about him. "You obviously can't handle being with me."

The ball went on, high spirits gathering momentum as the night wore on. Genni did her very best to try and match the festive mood but by half past one she had to concede defeat. When she left the hall with Lally—it was decided Colin would stay on he was having such a whale of a time—it was to see Blaine and Sally literally tucked away amid the potted palms enjoying what had to be very meaningful conversation. Sally looked unmistakeably a woman in love.

"Do you think Blaine and Sally will ever make a match of it?" Genni asked Lally, not fully aware of her dispirited tone.

"He's not in love with her, dear. You know that. I mean, it's been a kind of no-strings-attached relationship."

Genni gave the older woman a wry sidelong smile. "But she's in love with him, don't forget. She's hung in there. She's a really nice person. She would make him an excellent wife."

"In some respects, yes," Lally conceded. "Sally's Outback born and bred. She's a good strong healthy girl with a sensible head on her shoulders. There's joy in her, too. I like that, but she has no *pull,* if you know what I mean. A pull like the moon and the tide. It's a thing apart. I never had it. You do."

Genni shook her head. "Then I don't really want it. It hasn't worked for me, Lally, even if it were true. I've done something, too, I promised you I wouldn't."

"Go on. What?" Lally led the way into the homestead, looking faintly aghast.

"I made Blaine angry." Genni gave a brittle laugh. "Yet again. We don't have that simple loving relationship any more."

"You never did," Lally observed, gripped Genni's hand, looking into the lovely face that was showing strain. "Go to bed, sweetheart," she urged. "I'm praying the two of you will work it all out."

She fell asleep the minute her head hit the pillow despite her tangle of bittersweet emotions, and the sounds of merrymaking that continued for hours. It would have been understandable had she slept well into the morning but she awoke at first light, wanting to be out of doors. Out in the wild bush where she could think.

A small crowd of guests, who had never gone to bed, was enjoying a lavish buffet breakfast when she went downstairs. No sign of Colin. She waved a hand at those who caught sight of her then quietly slipped away through the back door on her way to the stables. There she saddled up Aurora, a lovely sweet-tempered exhilarating ride.

She made straight across the maze of gullies that lay between the homestead and its small township of satellite buildings and her favourite lagoon the family called The Isis. It had been named years ago by Blaine's great-grandfather, after the most important of the ancient Egyptian goddesses. Isis, Mother of all things, the lady of all the elements, the beginning of all time.

The name had sprung from the fact this glorious sheet of permanent water, the biggest lagoon on the station, bore the Blue Lotus, the sacred flower of ancient Egypt, in great abundance. It often seemed strange to Genni that this particular waterlily was native to both Australia and North Africa supporting the legends that had existed almost from the time of colonisation of an ancient Egyptian presence in Australia. So many relics had been unearthed in the tropics, artifacts of all kinds, gold coins, gold statues, scarabs, seals, jewellery. Fascinating! In the tomb of Tutakhamon golden boomerangs had been discovered. The boomerang was the Australian aborigine's traditional hunting weapon.

Genni rode on, her troubled feelings, frustration, anger, bewilderment, intense emotionalism eased by the beauty and freshness of the morning. As always the birds accompanied her on her journey, hundreds of little zebra finches, the favourite prey of the falcons and hawks, squadrons of budgerigar in their usual V-shaped formations. White corellas decorated the belt of red-barked trees that ran along the watercourse she took, in stark contrast to the brilliant plumage of the parrots that made their home in the avenues of acacias on the opposite banks. Even at this early hour the mirage was up and about with its extraordinary visual effects, sending a rolling sea of blue waves across the open grasslands where she could see a section of the herd grazing. She adored this desert country.

From an artistic viewpoint, and she hoped to become a good painter one day, there was infinite scope for her brush. The fiery intensity of colours thrilled her; the brilliant dry ochres, the contrasting blazing blue of the cloudless sky, the magnificent sculptural effects of the ancient rocks and monuments, the bleached-white skeletons of desert oaks, and the gnarled and twisted mulgas, the ripple textured, undulating red sand dunes that rolled across the desert like the fabled inland sea.

She loved the vastness of this sun-scorched land the lonely mesas and eroded plateaus, the great network of criss-crossing water channels, billabongs and lagoons that gave life to such a savagely parched area. But even in drought the desert had a majestic beauty. Then to make the spirits soar, after the rains, the miracle of the wildflowers when the entire desert landscape was transformed into a garden on the grandest scale on earth.

She loved Jubilee with a passion that matched Blaine's. The land spoke to her as it did to him. One of the things that had made them so close. Only what she *really* wanted from Blaine couldn't be hoped for. She couldn't even believe in it. There was no person in the world, including her mother, she loved as much as she loved Blaine. Absolutely nobody.

But after that…that…moment out of time, she had to recognise though she had been completely unprepared for it, her feelings had been…sexual. A fantasy. A rapid shift simply because he had looked at her with a different flavour. As a man looks at a woman. This manifestly was what had caused her growing feelings of frustration. The latent powerful urge towards Blaine as a lover.

Was she becoming her mother? Terrible thought. It couldn't

be denied both she and Blaine had become increasingly hostile at some level. He standing between her and the things she thought she wanted to do, she straining away from his authority. What was truly frightening was their once beautiful relationship might self-destruct. A thought not to be borne.

Coming down on the emerald lagoon Genni dismounted and led Aurora down the track with its ground cover of delicate little mauve flowers so pretty it was a pity to have to tread on them. Climbing wild passionfruit hung from the trees, the vines covered with a profusion of the pale pink cyclamen-centred flowers. It was wondrously peaceful. So quiet. A large area of the lagoon was floating huge green pads, rising above the leaves the gorgeous hyacinth blue of the lotus lilies. Flowering grasses and reeds fringed the banks, the golden blossoms of a native grevillea flourishing in the rocky terrain of the opposite bank.

Genni walked to the water's edge, bent to splash her heated face in the crystal-clear water, pure enough to drink. A flock of lily trotters were out on the water, some walking delicately on the lily pads, others resting on a raised platform of water grasses. Beautiful images she always carried in her heart.

Last night Colin had as good as asked her to marry him. Perhaps he would have got down on his knees and made a real proposal had she given him a bit more encouragement. But she had held back, no longer sure of anything. She could honestly say she had really enjoyed being with Colin these last months. He was so easy, so undemanding, whereas Blaine for instance was too demanding by far. Blaine was the yardstick for everyone. Add to that he didn't take her seriously. Genni turned away from the water and found a cool spot on the sand, lying back and resting her ash-blond head on her hat. She felt awfully low and it all had to do with you-know-who.

She was half asleep, gently drifting, when Blaine found her. He'd guessed where she was going when someone told him she'd been seen dressed in riding clothes. Genni loved The Isis. It was one of her favourite places on the station.

"Wake up, sleepyhead," he said gently, taking special care not to startle her. He went down on his haunches, brushing her cheek with a flowering frond of grass.

Her beautiful eyes flashed open, staring up into the dark handsome face above her. She wasn't in the least surprised he had found her. Blaine had always read her mind with perfect accuracy. The first rush of joy was replaced by a wariness that showed in her eyes.

"What a night!" Abruptly she sat up only to be further unsettled as he took up a position beside her on the sand.

"They're still partying, would you believe?" He took off his grey akubra and threw it unerringly atop a small nearby rock. "Couldn't you sleep?"

"Couldn't you?"

"Genni, dearest, have you forgotten I don't need much sleep."

"I'm sorry for the way I behaved last night," she said, under the benign influence of the bush.

"I thought you were rejoicing in your fast developing powers."

"I haven't grown up like you wanted, have I?" She spoke softly.

"Why ever would you say that?" His response was instant. Then he spoilt it. "You're still as adorable as ever I remember."

"You're a sarcastic devil, aren't you?" She shook her thick plait back over her shoulder.

"I am if it kills me," he said dryly. "But you're equal to it."

Genni was quiet for a moment trying to straighten things out in her mind. "I love this place," she eventually said.

"I know."

"There's a lot of countrywoman in me."

He gave her his beautiful heartbreaking smile. "I have all the memories, Genevieve."

"Have you? What happened to us, Blaine?"

"In what way?" He looked away across the glittering water.

"We don't communicate like we used to."

"Maybe you're growing up has something to do with it," he suggested.

"Is that what it is?" She spoke quietly. "Colin asked me to marry him last night."

The sensuous mouth twisted. "Do you suppose he'll remember this morning?"

"Can I speak seriously to you at all," she burst out, staring at his handsome profile, the determined jaw.

"Certainly. About *serious* things. If Colin was on the level and not merely half drunk I'd advise against it very strongly."

"Why?" Anger burned in her. "I've got to get married sometime."

"What a ridiculous answer."

"Why do you have to sound as if you're humouring a child?" She reached blindly for a stone and threw it at the water.

"Another example of arrogance," he asked, black-brown brows lifted.

"Well you are. When I seek your opinion you deliberately set out to crush me."

"Oh, Genni." His expression softened unexpectedly. "I can't take this seriously. Colin Garrett is not the man for you. And from where I'm sitting you're not even in love with him."

Awkwardly for such a graceful girl she sprang to her feet, her voice high and defiant. "How would you know?"

"Because I *know* you."

He, too, came to his feet, towering over her like some damned skyscraper, she thought. They faced each other. "What are you trying to prove anyway?" he asked. "That you'd do anything to distance yourself from me and my world?"

She was genuinely shocked. "How can you say that?"

"Maybe it's true." His expression turned dark and broody.

"Can't I have anyone else, Blaine?" she pleaded. "Can't I love anyone else? You treat me as though I'm still a child. Colin treats me like a woman. That alone is fantastic after you all the time. Now he's asked me to marry him and I'm thinking about marrying him."

The silver gaze was torched. "If you do anything so *stupid*, so *ill-advised*, I don't think I'd ever want to see you again."

"You can't mean that?" She fell back a little in her dismay.

"I'm a hard man, remember." He held her gaze.

"I know the way your mother abandoned you has never left your mind." She trembled as she said it.

"But I did recover, didn't I, Genni?" He gave a thin smile. "What makes you think I can't recover from you?"

She bit her lip so hard she tasted blood. "Oh, this is so painful, so painful, this taste of bitterness."

"It's a by-product of what's happening between us," he retaliated. "Somewhere in your mind, Genni, you have to discover the truth."

"Maybe the truth is so complicated to bear." She put up her hands swiftly to cup her flushed face.

"There's hardly anything to feel guilty about," he said sharply.

"And what about you?" she challenged him. "You interfere in all my relationships. I never say one word about yours."

"Come on," he jibed, "that's not true." Suddenly amused, but darkly relentless. "Remember Marsha and Sophie?"

"I only remember cracking a few jokes you used to laugh at. Lord, I couldn't even count the number of women in your life. I can't even understand how one of them hasn't grabbed you."

"You're kidding! I wouldn't allow them." He stretched out a hand but she jumped back, pink-cheeked, her breath catching in her throat.

"I'm going to marry Colin." She said it like it was her last defence against him.

"Excuse me, you're *not*. You're not ready for marriage. Especially one that would never work."

"Sez you!" She felt like a woman possessed, unable to control her excitement and anger. "Colin makes me feel like a woman."

"The hell he does!" His voice rasped in her ears, as he looked at her his remarkable eyes full of disgust.

"Anyone can make you feel like a woman," he ground out.

Mutely, knowing what was coming, as vulnerable as a baby, she shook her head, her brain reeling as he did the sheerly unthinkable. He pulled her into his arms with stunning strength, binding her to him, his striking face taut and full of an inner struggle.

She tried to shake herself free of his iron grasp and found it impossible. She had always felt so safe with him, so secure. This would end everything. "Blaine, what are you doing?"

"Just what you think."

And it seemed to her perhaps she always knew what was coming. But how did she endure it? A punishment so exquisite it was a life-changing experience. It was passion. Pure, hopeless, unbridled passion. It raged around them like a great conflagration. She had never in her life felt his mouth moulding hers, opening it, like a man not to be denied, his tongue sliding over her teeth, moving in deep exploration. She had never felt his arms pinning her body. It was ecstasy and violation. He might just reach her soul. The violence of the kiss went on, never losing its blazing energy. It conveyed his old love for her and his present contempt.

When his hand slipped to her breast, claiming it with sovereign mastery, it seemed like a monumental symbolic act. It startled her out of her mind. Enveloped her in such heat her blood felt like lava. She thought she would slip to the ground only he held her so forcefully, intent on demonstrating his physical and sexual supremacy.

He did it brilliantly. She couldn't survive this. She was

exposed. One after another Blaine was stripping away all the veils she had worn since she was a child.

She whispered his name with her last breath, conscious his mouth and hands relented at last.

He looked down at her, her lovely pale face, her closed, shadowed eyes, the pulsing rose coloured cushioned mouth. A muscle clenching and unclenching along his strong jaw.

Facing the truth is never easy. Sometimes an unforeseen tragedy could strike. He had thought to liberate Genni from all her confusions but he had only disturbed her further. Worse, terrified her. He had never touched her breasts. Unthinkable. His caressing hand had so shocked her it had filtered through even his mad recklessness. The perfume of her was in his nostrils. It wrapped around him like a cloud.

And now she was stumbling away from him, at first unable to speak, then crying out she hated him, how he oppressed her, near hysterical with shock.

Women how they could destroy a man!

CHAPTER FIVE

The Day After The Wedding That Almost Was

GENNI felt very remorseful when she got off the phone. Remorseful and very sad. What she would really like to do was disappear off the face of the earth. That was Colin. Complaining at the beginning he hadn't been able to speak to her earlier simply because he couldn't get through. That had been Angel. Still nursing the forlorn hope the marriage would go ahead.

Genni had told her no, which led to her mother becoming very angry and calling her "heartless." That from Angel. A classic case of the pot calling the kettle black.

But she had opened up her feelings to Colin. He was kind and in his own way sensitive. A very nice human being who would grow if he could only break away from his dreadful father. She had cried. Colin had cried. In the end both vowing to stay friends forever. It wasn't everyday a jilted bridegroom actually said, "Forget it" when she tried to express her shame, her remorse, her gratitude to him for hearing her out. She had behaved very very badly but Colin convinced her he understood, causing her affection for him, for that was what it *was,* to rise meteorically. Colin had a way with women. Even as she put down the phone, the tears streaming down her cheeks,

Genni just knew he wouldn't have the slightest difficulty finding the next. Perhaps that very afternoon.

He hadn't even asked about the engagement ring but of course she would return it. "The monstrosity," Lally had called it. Likewise to be returned the mountain of wedding gifts still on display at Angel's. Instead of using a carrier service perhaps the guests could collect their particular wedding present when they called in on Angel again. Tiffany had told her on the phone with many wicked laughs the "reception" had gone off very well. "You should have been there!" Which was positively weird. Only Tiffany had divined where her heart lay.

Genni dragged herself out of the narrow hospital bed and went into the shower. Darling Em had showed up first thing with a change of clothes for her, so light-hearted one would have thought far from making an exhibition of herself Genni had done something highly commendable. Like marry the Right Man.

She was dressed and waiting when Blaine arrived, putting down the glossy magazine she had been pretending to read. No doubt she would be asked to contribute an article to that very magazine in the near future, citing a nervous breakdown.

"Ready?" So he greeted her, this man who had put her through hell. He was casually dressed in a very sharp red-and-navy open-necked sports shirt with navy jeans, so handsome, so virile, so Blaine, the tears spilled over again. "Come on, Genni. We've got to get through this," he responded with a touch of asperity. No pats on the head. "Dry the tears. Better you feel miserable than having made a hideous mistake."

Wasn't that the truth! "I can't bear to go home. I can not," she appealed to him. "Angel thinks it's still on."

"Angel's ambition has always been to marry you off to the wrong man. I'm not taking you back to your mother, cherub. I'm taking you over to my hotel. To Lally. We fly back to Jubilee this afternoon. I want you to come."

All around her the cymbals clanged. "I suppose you couldn't tell me you *want* me to come," she begged. "You're not simply helping me to hide from the world?"

"Work it out." He picked up her one small case, taking her arm and leading her out of the room. He seemed in an awful hurry, long legs moving like an athlete in training.

"What about the bill?" she prompted him at reception.

"That's all taken care of. You've told Colin, haven't you?"

"Why do you think I was crying?" she sighed.

"Making big mistakes and learning from them can be character building," he pointed out very dryly.

"Blast you. You're the one who said I had no character to begin with."

They were at the front door when Blaine drew back, staring down at her, brow knitted. "A couple of photographers are outside. I just bet they're waiting for us."

"And I just hope you've got a car." She tried to see around his shoulder. "A *fast* car."

"Your BMW, as it happens."

She looked up at him, her violet eyes huge. "That'll do. We'll walk out nonchalantly."

"Great!" he jeered, his eyes sweeping over her sensational in a simple pink dress. "Put your sunglasses on and don't speak."

It was like running a red light.

Lally had the finest suite in the hotel but when they arrived, Lally, who had spoken to Genni earlier, was nowhere to be found.

"A note here," Blaine read out the few lines jotted down on the hotel notepaper. "Gone off on an errand. Back in an hour."

"Well," said Genni with an enormous effort, sinking into a plush sofa. "Can we talk? *Privately.* I think that's Lally's intention."

"I thought you found talking to me difficult," he countered, making no move towards her.

"I know I upset you." She hung her white-gold head.

Only then he reacted. "Hell, Genni, I've had to take as much as a man can take. You realize you nearly married Colin."

"Yes, yes!" she shuddered. "I was like out of control."

"It's time you grew up."

"I know. I've made a fool of Colin."

Blaine swivelled towards the balcony that looked out on the magnificent blue harbour. "The truth is he's none too bright. Or even faithful. Cancelled wedding or not I believe your Colin had a great time last night."

Genni nearly said, "Who cares!" but stopped in time. "Colin's like that," she said tolerantly. "Anyway, he was very noble."

Blaine shot her a sparkling admonishing look. "Oh, shut up."

"Okay I will. But before I do I want to tell you I love you," she cried emotionally. "I love you in every way possible. I was just hysterical that time you kissed me. The *one* time you kissed me like that. But it blew me away. I kept bumping into things for weeks."

Blaine walked back and lowered himself into an armchair near her. "How can a woman be so perverse? You acted like being kissed was life-threatening."

"It is. It *was*. From you. I must be terribly naive, I wasn't ready for a sexual encounter. We've been family. You've treated me almost like your sister then you throw me in the deep end. In a way it was a kind of terror." She extended her hand to him, her heart in her eyes. "Blaine, I need you. I need you like no one else on earth."

"As what?" His brilliant eyes swept her face.

"You want a quick answer?" Lights seemed to be spilling inside her head.

"I'll never kiss you again if I don't get it."

"It's crazy," she exclaimed, her violet eyes ardent, "but I want to be your wife. *Your wife*. No one else's."

"No matter how dangerous?" Now he moved, lithe as a panther, sitting down beside her and pulling her across his knees.

She stared up at him. So familiar. The most familiar face in the world. Any yet… "Give me a minute to think."

"No! No! No!" Like a man at the end of his tether, Blaine lowered his head, one hand cupping her delicate skull, holding her tantalizing mouth up to him.

He needn't have bothered. This time Genni was ready. As Blaine dipped his mouth to kiss her she lifted her head to meet him inviting the rapturous crush of desire. Her soul took wings. All the barriers were down. All the deep running, hidden yearnings out in the open.

It was a fever of want that both submitted to, both muttering endearments against the other's tongue. His arms cradled her; one of her arms lay trembling around his neck.

"My Blaine. My Blaine." She murmured his name over and over, her voice shaking with emotion. His broad hand moved to the tilted curve of her breast and she arched her back in desperation overcome by desire. Her skin felt as if it were burning. She had had no idea about love. Now she was beginning to understand… to understand the ecstasy.

"Your heart is in my hands," he whispered passionately, taking the tender weight of her breast.

"I love you. No one else," she whispered back, feeling his mouth brush warmly across her throat before returning to her mouth, his kiss so voluptuous, so dominating…so authoritative…so full of a lifetime's tenderness.

"You're going to marry me. Is that understood?" Briefly he lifted his raven head.

"You want it in writing?" She thought she was dissolving in bliss.

"Not really." His smile held the same old mocking charm. "This time, Violetta, you'll get it right."